'This is an action-packed adventure that will take you on a ride... There is fast-paced drama in each chapter, which keeps you gripped to the story. I love the historical element...'
The Teacher Bookworm, teacher blogger

'Full of great characters — both horses and humans — and Dido is a terrific heroine... Annelise Gray has written a story that is both historically convincing and heart-stoppingly exciting. I hope there are more to come.'
Gillian Cross, author of The Demon Headmaster series

'Lovers of history, horses and heart-stopping adventure will be gripped by this action-packed and fast-paced read which will sweep you off your feet, leave you breathless and wanting to know more of the history behind the fiction.'
Armadillo

'Gray transports the reader to Rome in a hoofbeat, places, people and the dangerous times vividly brought to life... A superb historical adventure story.'
LoveReading

'It's fantastic... I loved it and there's a sequel to look forward to also.'
Anne Thompson, The Library Lady, blogger

CIRCUS
MAXIMUS
Race to the Death

CIRCUS MAXIMUS

Race to the Death

ANNELISE GRAY

ZEPHYR

An imprint of Head of Zeus

First published in the UK by Zephyr,
an imprint of Head of Zeus, in 2021

9 7 5 3 1 2 4 6 8

A catalogue record for this book is available
from the British Library.

ISBN (PB): 9781800240582
ISBN (E): 9781800240599

Typesetting & design by Ed Pickford

Printed and bound in Great Britain
by CPI Group (UK) Ltd, Croydon CR0 4YY

Head of Zeus Ltd
First Floor East
5–8 Hardwick Street
London EC1R 4RG

WWW.HEADOFZEUS.COM

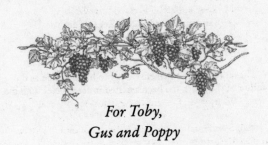

For Toby,
Gus and Poppy

Cast of Characters

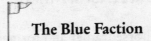

The Green Faction
Rome's most popular chariot racing team

Antonius – the head trainer for the Greens

Dido – twelve-year-old daughter of Antonius

Atticus – assistant trainer to Antonius

Hosidius Ruga – the faction master

Justus – Ruga's nephew

Darius and Scylax – brothers and hard-bitten charioteers

Fuscus – a less illustrious charioteer

The Blue Faction

Opellius Otho – the wealthiest of the four faction masters at Rome

Helvia – Otho's observant wife

Fabius – a famous and handsome charioteer

Crito – the head trainer for the Blues

Helix – a veteran charioteer

Betucius Barus – an investor in the Blue faction

Corinna – a slave-girl

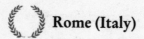 **Rome (Italy)**

Caligula – great-nephew and heir to Emperor Tiberius

Drusilla – Caligula's sister

Naevius Sutorius Macro – Prefect of the Praetorian Guard (the emperor's personal bodyguard)

Ennia – a daughter of Macro

Rufus, Mathos and Abascantus – a trio of sailors

Cassius Chaerea – a soldier in the Praetorian Guard

Charicles – a doctor in the emperor's household

 Utica (North Africa)

Scorpus – a racehorse trainer and former charioteer

Hanno and Abibaal – Scorpus's young sons

Anna – a slave-girl in Scorpus's household

Nicias – a brilliant but brutal apprentice charioteer

Parmenion – a friend of Nicias and also a talented charioteer

Antigonus – an apprentice charioteer who lets his driving do the talking

Gisco – a horse dealer in the market at Carthage

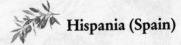

Hispania (Spain)

Marius – a racehorse trainer and friend of Antonius

Teres – son of Marius

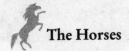

The Horses

Porcellus – a fiery black stallion

Boreas, Eurus, Auster and Zephyr (the Four Winds) – the greatest four-horse team in the empire

Nessus – an inside horse for the Greens

Icarus – a blue roan with a heart of gold

Sciron – the toughest horse in Scorpus's stable

Perdix, Hannibal, Mago, Snowy and Iris – more horses from Scorpus's stable

Patch, Lightning, Swift and Silver – a Blue faction four

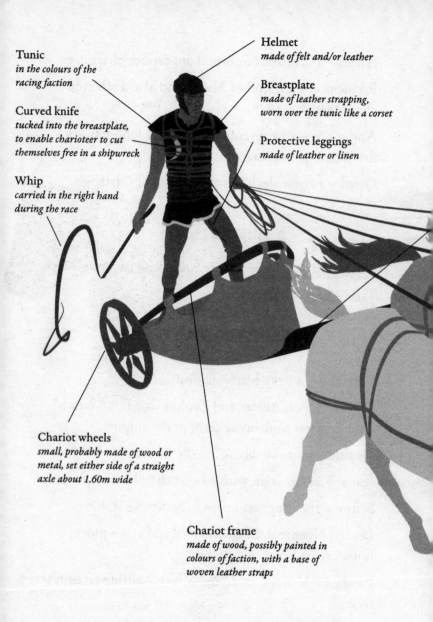

Tunic
in the colours of the racing faction

Curved knife
tucked into the breastplate, to enable charioteer to cut themselves free in a shipwreck

Whip
carried in the right hand during the race

Helmet
made of felt and/or leather

Breastplate
made of leather strapping, worn over the tunic like a corset

Protective leggings
made of leather or linen

Chariot wheels
small, probably made of wood or metal, set either side of a straight axle about 1.60m wide

Chariot frame
made of wood, possibly painted in colours of faction, with a base of woven leather straps

No racing chariot remains have survived the journey through time from the Roman world. This sketch is based on research into images of chariot racing in ancient art and literature.

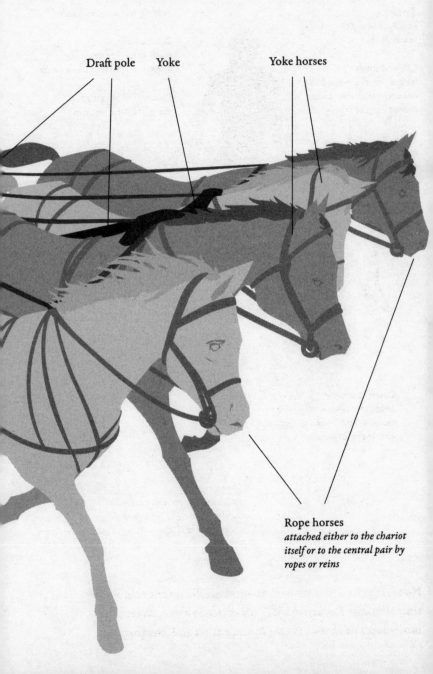

Draft pole Yoke Yoke horses

Rope horses
*attached either to the chariot
itself or to the central pair by
ropes or reins*

I

'Ready?'

My spit left a mark in the soft red earth. Teres grinned and waved towards the boy perching in the olive tree on the far side of the plain. The boy raised his arm and Teres's friends sitting on the fence started to clap. I kept my eyes on the white cloth rippling from the branches of the tree. It swooped suddenly and there was a crack as Teres's whip came down.

'Get up!'

I slapped the reins across the backs of my two roans. Their rusty bellies were swollen from a long day out in the pasture, and it took seven or eight strides to get them into a canter. We lumbered along the strip of track, my chariot's wheels bumping over the churned earth in Teres's wake. *Keep your head, don't push too early.* Teres's greys were rounding the olive tree. He shouted at me as he accelerated past in the other direction.

'You see? I told you those two weren't that fast!'

I pulled hard on the left rein to make my inside roan chop his stride as we took the turn. The twine at the nape of my neck flew off and my hair whipped across my face like straw. I could see my father, Antonius, hurrying down the sloping side of the valley from the stable yard.

'Dido, stop!'

I didn't look at him. At the opposite turn – round an old fence-post – Teres was careless, veering wide and losing some of his advantage. What had I heard Antonius tell the Green charioteers a thousand times? *The turn is the most important part of the race.* I steered the roans on the quickest line possible, then let them have their heads as we tore towards the olive tree. Their muddy necks flexed like a pair of catapults. The vibrations shaking the chariot made my knees buckle. I tried hard not to think about what would happen if one of my wheels suddenly went over a rock. I'd seen broken charioteers before, their necks at a strange angle, their skin shredded to the raw red below. My mother's silver charm danced in the hollow of my throat. Dust spun by Teres's wheels drifted back down the plain. I closed my eyes against the oncoming rush of warm sand.

When I opened them again, I could see the sweat coating the ends of Teres's dark hair. His greys were tiring badly after being driven too fast on that first lap, their necks dipping lower. We were coming to the olive tree for the second and final time. Teres sensed the threat behind him and lashed the greys with his whip. His chariot slid wide around the tree, throwing up a fan of earth. He swore loudly as I stole the inside line.

'I told you those two wouldn't last the distance!' I shouted at him.

Teres's friends were standing on the fence, cheering him on. Neck and neck, we raced towards the finish. My eyes were streaming and my legs on fire with the pain of keeping my knees bent. The boy who had started our race from the olive tree was now standing on the old fence-post, holding the white cloth in the air once more. I brought up my arm.

One flick of the whip ought to do it.

Startled by my sudden strike, the roans lifted their tails and their heads came up. I streaked past the boy waving the cloth and punched my fist in the air.

By the time I managed to get the roans under control, I could see Antonius waiting for me, the sun glinting on his golden head. Alongside him was Teres's father, Marius. The boys were swarming around Teres, laughing and patting him on the back.

'You lost to a girl,' one of them was saying and they all started repeating the insult.

Antonius came forward.

'Did you see, Papa? I won!' I tried to sound as though I expected him to share my enthusiasm.

'I saw. Get down from there. What do you think you're playing at, Dido? You could have killed yourself!'

I stepped down, running my hand along the inside roan's flank as I approached his head.

'Don't get angry, Papa. You know I've driven lots of times at the practice track back home.'

'That's not the same thing as risking your neck in a real race!' Antonius's green eyes were blazing. 'You want to die before your thirteenth birthday? Or end up like Lepidus, after he got shipwrecked? Is that what you want, Dido? To see your bones breaking through your flesh?'

'No,' I muttered. 'But it's not as if we were driving fours, just pairs. Teres said I could pick whichever horses I wanted from their yard. I knew he'd go for fast ones and push them too hard. All I had to do was keep to a good line and control the pace.' I patted the ponies' damp necks. 'I thought if I did everything the way you taught me, I'd do well.'

To my relief, Antonius's face relaxed a little.

'You did do well. If I hadn't been so terrified,

I might have been able to enjoy it.' He put a hand on the back of my head and made me look at him. 'But never ever frighten me like that again, you hear me?'

My beaten opponent approached, his friends now crowded on to the axle alongside him. The greys were blowing their flanks in exhaustion. Teres had lost some of his swagger though he was still grinning.

'Good race. What do you say, best of three?'

'Forget it. We had a deal, now you have to pay up.'

'Stop right there, Dido,' said Antonius. 'If you think I'm going to let you make money out of doing something so stupid, you can think again.'

'No, you don't understand, Papa. We weren't racing for money.'

'I see. What, dare I ask, *was* the stake?'

I hesitated.

'If I won, she'd have to give us all a kiss,' said Teres. '*All* of us.' He jerked his thumb back to his friends who beamed.

Antonius raised an eyebrow at me.

'And if *you* won?' he asked.

I turned and pointed.

'I get *him*.'

Antonius looked up at the little black horse grazing alone in the field above the plain. He was a young stallion, about four years old, with a white star in the middle of his forehead. His long tail swished as he plucked at the few patches of green. Encouragingly, I could see Antonius assessing the fine head, powerful shoulders and sturdy fetlocks, ideal for withstanding the break-neck turns of a chariot-race.

'Look at him, Papa! Isn't he beautiful? Teres says he was a gift from his father, but he doesn't want him any more. He's made to be an inside horse, don't you think? I can just see him taking the turns at the Circus Maximus.'

Someone snorted with laughter.

'The Circus? Sure, sure, if you can get him in the starting gate.'

Marius was waddling over with a bucket of water. Setting it down for the roans and greys to dip their greedy muzzles into, he wiped the sweat from his broad forehead.

'Well done, Dido. You've taught this boy of mine a lesson in race craft, one I hope he'll remember if he ever gets to the Circus.' He gave Teres a friendly slap on the head. 'But it's a poor stake he's offered you.'

He nodded at my father.

'Don't get me wrong, Antonius, there's good blood in that animal. Sired him out of a Libyan stallion I put with one of my best mares. I expected to get a fortune for that little black horse whenever you or the next lot of faction scouts came by. That was before I knew his temperament. Broke three chariots when we first tried to get him in harness, not to mention my groom's arm. I thought it might teach Teres something, trying to bring him on. But he can't handle him, none of my boys can.' He put a hand on my shoulder. 'Don't lose your heart to that horse, my girl. He's a Fury.'

'But he isn't! Watch.'

I ducked under the fence and climbed the slope to where the black horse was grazing. He lifted his head, watching me with nostrils flared, ears twitching. Slipping my hand into the pouch pocket of my old green tunic, I extracted a dusty handful of grain. Holding it on the tips of my fingers, I whispered and cooed as I shuffled forward. A squeal escaped the horse's throat and he tossed his mane, dancing on the spot. I stopped a few paces short of his head, arm still outstretched, and made the same squealing noise he had made. The little black horse stared. Then he stretched out his nose, sniffing at the grain. Blowing softly, he took a few cautious steps towards me. His upper lip brushed against my palm and he began snaffling the grain, tickling my fingers with his whiskers. He flinched slightly when I began stroking his cheek.

'I don't believe it,' I heard Marius say to Antonius. 'Can she talk to horses, that girl of yours?'

The fence creaked as someone climbed over it. The little horse's ears flattened against his skull. I tried to soothe him by combing his long mane with my fingers. Antonius stopped a short distance away. I knew what was coming.

'Dido, we didn't come all this way to Hispania to buy an untrained horse.'

'We're not buying him. I won him.'

'I have my orders from Ruga. The Greens need to start winning races again. If we're to have any chance of beating the Blues, we need fully trained animals, horses that have experience of the local circuses.'

'I'll train him. You can help me. Please, Papa.'

'And what do I tell Ruga when he asks why I've wasted a place in the boat's cargo on a horse that has never run a race? A horse whose upkeep he'll have to pay for?'

'Tell him he had too much promise to leave behind. Tell him what Marius said about his sire, tell him…'

I stopped. Even to my ears, it sounded unconvincing. I knew the master of the Green faction as well as my father did. Ruga was as tight-fisted as he was wealthy.

Antonius held out his hand. The lump in my throat had swollen to the size of a stone. I buried my face in the horse's neck, breathing in his warm, sweet smell. Then I let my father take my hand and lead me back to the fence. Through my tears, I could see Teres looking at me curiously.

'Dido and I have a long journey ahead of us. We should set off tonight if we're to make it to Tarraco in time for the morning boat. My thanks for your hospitality, Marius. Superb choice of horses as always. I think Ruga will be especially pleased with those new chestnuts. You'll send them on?'

'Of course, Antonius, my old friend. They'll be on the next transport over. I hope they help revive the Greens' fortunes.'

'I hope so too. Or Ruga may start looking for another trainer.'

There was a pause. I felt Antonius's hand tighten on mine.

'Out of interest, what would you take for the little black horse, Marius?'

My eyes went to my father's face. What I saw there made my heart almost burst with love for him. Marius chuckled.

'I'd say you're welcome to him, Antonius, and good luck to you if you think you can make anything of him. I won't take your money, you're too good a friend for me to cheat you. But the horse is Teres's to give.'

I looked at Teres, who glanced in turn at the little black horse. I knew that he was wondering whether he was making a mistake in giving up something someone else wanted so badly. Then his teeth gleamed white.

'You earned him. Take him if you want him.'

He leaned forward and pointed to his cheek.

'Now what do you say?'

I wavered. Then I planted a quick kiss on his brown jaw. The boys behind him cheered.

II

'You missed a bit, Justus. There, down by his fetlock.'

'Oh, don't be so fussy, Dido, no one's going to notice that.' Justus pushed his dark hair off his forehead.

'Do it.' I finished tying the last green ribbon into Nessus's mane and stepped down off the upturned bucket to inspect them proudly. I was known at the stables for the neatness of my plaiting. 'Papa won't be happy unless everything is perfect.'

'Who's in charge here, my uncle or your father?'

'My father, as it happens. Your uncle may own the faction, but in the stables, Antonius's word is law. Ruga sent you here to learn, so get brushing.'

Justus rolled his eyes, but I could tell he wasn't really offended by my ordering him about. Most boys would be, especially when they were three years older. It was one of the nice things about

Justus. I gave Nessus's coat one last brush then took a hoof-pick from the grooming bucket and clicked my tongue to encourage him to lift his foot. To my surprise, he kicked out.

'Hey. What's the matter, boy?'

Nessus swished his tail angrily.

'Maybe he thinks his feet are clean enough,' suggested Justus.

I was about to say something rude in reply when I noticed what was happening by the Blues' stables opposite.

'Look, look, Justus, look!'

I jumped up on to the half-door of the stall, balancing on my elbows. Outside was the usual race-day scene of chaotic activity. Grooms from all the four factions – Reds, Whites, Blues and Greens – were scurrying across the Forum Boarium, bringing out horses in pairs and teams of four from the Circus stables. A stench lingered in the air from the piles of uncleared dung. Glossy with water and sweat, the horses were twitching as they eyeballed the crowds, their nostrils opening and closing like bellows as they were hitched into harness. Chariot engineers held whispered conferences, testing baskets with their weight, tightening axles, shortening reins. Vets watched critically as horses were given a final walk-out in front of them.

But none of that interested me right now. Everyone in the forum, even the Green supporters, was watching the stables opposite ours, which were being used by our great rivals, the Blues. A man wearing a close-fitting helmet over his long curly black hair and a breastplate of leather strapping over his blue tunic had emerged from the drivers' changing room and was holding up his hand to acknowledge the cheers of the Blues' supporters.

'It's Fabius! The Blues' number one. Four hundred and fifty-two victories, two hundred and seventy-six second places and a hundred and twelve third places from one thousand and eighty-six races. Come over here, Justus, you have to see this.'

A team of four tight-muscled chestnut horses were being led out and prepared for harness. Their coats seemed to ripple like water in the sunlight, blue ribbons streaming from their flaxen manes and tails. I leaned out as far as I could and pointed for Justus's benefit.

'Boreas, Auster, Eurus and Zephyr. Otherwise known as the Four Winds. The greatest racehorses in the whole empire.' The biggest of the four surged forward, dragging the groom holding him to the ground. 'That's Boreas. See how strong he is? It's what makes him such a good outside rope horse.

Any other team tries to steal their racing line and he just shoulders them off.'

'Remind me again, what's the difference between a rope horse and a yoke horse?' asked Justus. I groaned in disbelief.

'I can't believe you still haven't got this. How are you going to run the faction one day? The yoke horses go in the middle and they give you your rhythm and power, that's Eurus and Auster going into harness now. The rope horses are tethered to the chariot by traces on the outside and inside. They're the ones with the foot speed.'

'And the inside horse is the most important one? That's the one whose name the crowd cheers?'

'Yes, that's Zephyr, just going in last now. Isn't he gorgeous? The best inside horse he's ever seen, Papa says. Though my little Porcellus is going to change his mind. You didn't see us in the practice arena the other day, Justus. It's only been a month since he arrived from Hispania and already I can get him to turn on a coin. I can't believe Teres didn't want him. He's so clever and full of mischief. He likes to pretend he's being well-behaved while I'm hitching him to the draft pole but then he'll take off as I'm about to step on to the chariot. He always comes back, though, and nudges me to say he's sorry. I don't even have to put a rope on him when we bring the horses in from the pasture, he just follows me back to the stable. Oh, here goes Fabius – look, Justus, see the way he handles the reins? He drives with such a light hand.'

As Fabius drove past the Green stables towards the warm-up arena alongside the Circus, I got a good view of his face, with its full lips and laughing eyes. He saw me watching him and with a grin, he lifted his arm in salute and winked. In my embarrassment, I slipped off the stable door.

'Such a light hand,' said Justus, a far-off look in his eyes. 'Oh, he's so handsome… Ow!'

He rubbed his forehead where I'd hit him with the grooming brush. Nessus shied as it rebounded near his feet.

'Oh, Nessus, poor darling, I'm sorry. You are on edge today. I don't know what's the matter with you.' I went to calm the quivering horse, stroking his neck and kissing his muzzle. 'It's all Justus's fault.'

I finished getting Nessus ready just as Antonius arrived.

'All set?'

'Yes,' I said confidently as he inspected Nessus.

'I suppose I know where you want to go now.'

'I don't have to, if you need me here,' I said, trying not to sound insincere.

Antonius sighed. 'Is it any use pointing out he races for a rival faction?'

'Not really.'

'Go on then, you've both worked hard today. But come straight back here afterwards to help us take the horses up to the club-house, Dido – you hear me?'

I kissed my father's cheek.

'Thank you, Papa. It is the last race of the day, after all. By the way, watch out for Nessus, he's in an odd mood. He tried to kick me as I was picking out his feet.'

Antonius frowned.

'A lot of them have been playing up today. They're like cats on hot embers.'

There was a rumble of laughter behind us.

'Who cares? They're winning, aren't they?'

I turned to see the massive figure of my father's assistant trainer, Atticus, who was smiling at us over the stable door. His brow was covered in sweat and strands of his curly brown hair were sticking to his reddened cheeks.

'Nice plaits, Dido. You're learning from the best here, young Justus. She could teach every groom in this stable a thing or two. Not to mention some of the drivers. You'll be the first girl to race at the Circus Maximus someday, won't you, Dido?'

'Don't put silly ideas into her head, Atticus,' said Antonius.

'Why shouldn't he?' I demanded. 'It's stupid that I'm not allowed.'

'Keep dreaming, Dido.' Antonius nodded to Atticus. 'What happened in that last race?'

'What do you think? We won, of course. That's seven wins out of eleven so far. Not bad, eh?'

Antonius shook his head.

'None of our horses have shown this kind of form in training. Why are they all running well today? I wish I knew what I was doing right.'

'Hurry up, Dido, or we'll miss it!'

Justus was waiting for me half-way across the forum. As I ran after him, I collided with someone.

'Sorry!'

The man didn't answer. He was small and bald and wore a Green race-engineer's uniform. As I watched him walk away, I thought how clean and unsweaty he was compared to everyone else. His face wasn't familiar to me. Antonius must have taken on someone new.

'Come on, Dido!'

The engineer slipped out of my mind and I hurried after Justus.

III

Red, green, white and blue banners rippled like the tails of galloping horses from the buildings lining the forum. As Justus and I squeezed through the crowd, the delicious smell of hot sausages, fried oysters and salted peas tempted us, but we pressed on. Ahead, on the other side of the forum, loomed the great curving wall of the Circus Maximus itself. From its belly, full-throated roars were filling the sky, echoing like air rushing through a seashell.

By the warm-up arena, a crowd packed three or four deep watched the chariots preparing for the next race.

'That's Opellius Otho,' I said, pointing out a large man dressed head-to-toe in sky blue and flashing fat gold rings on his fingers, as he talked to a group of men in purple-striped tunics. 'He owns the Blues.'

'Is he the one my uncle calls the stink-merchant?'

'That's him. He's unbelievably wealthy, much more so than your Uncle Ruga, I'm afraid, which is probably why Ruga hates him. He made his fortune importing wine and fish sauce. Papa says he doesn't know a thing about horses but he's a good businessman. So there's hope for you yet.'

The chariots circling the warm-up arena were starting to gather around some stewards standing beside a large urn. I tugged the arm of Justus's tunic.

'Quick, they're about to draw for lanes. If we go this way, we might find a good seat...'

'Wait. Uncle Ruga. I think he's seen us.'

I let go of Justus's sleeve. Standing next to one of the passageways that led into the Circus, and talking to a burly, shaven-headed man in a plain white tunic, was the tall figure of the Greens' owner, Hosidius Ruga. He always reminded me of a wolf, with his greying pelt of hair and thick eyebrows which were now drawn close together. Ruga seemed unhappy about something the man in the white tunic was saying. But he was beckoning to us at the same time and put a hand on Justus's shoulder as he reached him. I kept a respectful distance, my gaze lowered.

'Justus, I want you to meet Sutorius Macro, Prefect of the Praetorian Guard.'

'Good-looking boy. Doesn't take after you, Ruga.'

'Justus is my late brother's son. He arrived in the city a few months ago. He'll take over the faction from me, one day.'

'Is that so?' Macro squinted at Justus with interest.

'I hope you don't mind my asking, but is Emperor Tiberius here for the races?' asked Justus. 'I thought he never left Capri.'

'He doesn't,' said Macro. 'Thinks someone's going to leap at him with a knife.' He made a sudden stabbing motion at Justus, who jumped. Macro laughed. 'Even though I'm here to look after him. It's a shame. The people like to see their emperor. But his great-nephew's here. Loves his racing, does Caligula. What about you, lad? Got a favourite charioteer?'

'To tell the truth, I don't yet,' admitted Justus. 'My father didn't really approve of racing. I've got a lot to learn, but Dido's helping me.'

I kept my eyes firmly on the ground.

'This little lady must be Dido. Who's she, your girlfriend?'

Ruga laughed in a way that showed he didn't think this was funny and answered for Justus.

'Hardly. Dido's father, Antonius, is my trainer.'

'Oh. Pretty, isn't she. All that golden hair with that bronze skin... like a little lioness...'

Macro stroked my cheek in a way I didn't like.

'Nice meeting you, lad,' he said to Justus. 'I've got a daughter I'd like to introduce you to one of these days. Ruga, good to run into you.'

He strolled away. His frown deepening, Ruga turned to Justus.

'Where are you two going in such a hurry?'

'Dido's taking me to see a race, Uncle.'

I could sense suspicion in Ruga's searching look, and I knew he didn't like the appearance of a friendship between Justus and me. But he nodded and we headed up a steep staircase that led to the top rows of the Circus. Squeezing past a long line of spectators, we were lucky to find one of the last gaps on the packed wooden benches, next to a noisy family of Green supporters.

I gazed into the crater of the Circus, the unpleasantness of the meeting with Macro and Ruga fading fast. The steep tiers of seating were splashed with red and white and larger bands of blue where supporters of those factions were seated together, their clothing uniting them in their tribes. But it was obvious which was the most popular faction. The whole of our side of the Circus was a wall of green. Down on the long oval floor of the stadium, sand rippled like a yellow river around the channel, the stone barrier dividing one side of the track from the other. Its entire length was decorated with statues, water fountains and soaring columns. Bronze pillars towered into the sky at either end where the charioteers had to make their turn. An official was pulling at the rope that hoisted the seven gold dolphins which would nose-dive one after the other during the race, to signal how many laps had been completed. Other stewards were raking smooth the sand while water boys from the different factions were getting into position along the channel, ready to jump down with their buckets and throw water over any chariot axles that looked to be overheating. I'd often begged Antonius to let me join them, but he said it was too dangerous and that water boys often got trampled.

Justus tapped me on the arm.

'Look. That's Caligula. Tiberius's heir.'

Shielding my eyes from the sun, I squinted at the emperor's private box which rose like a temple from the sea of spectators to our left. A tall, slender figure emerged on to the balcony and raised an arm in salute to the crowd. I could only see the back of his head. But I immediately noticed the colour he was wearing.

'He supports the Greens!' I said.

'Looks like it.'

'I like him, then. Why is he the heir if he's only the emperor's great-nephew?'

'The emperor doesn't have any sons of his own.' Justus lowered his voice. 'My father told me a story about Caligula once. When he was a little boy, he brought a real blade instead of a wooden one to a sword-fighting lesson and killed his trainer. Apparently he loves shows and spectacles and often dresses up as if he's a charioteer or a gladiator. My father thought that he—'

A blast of trumpets interrupted, and I lost interest in what Justus was saying.

'It's starting, it's starting! Here we go, just you wait until you see this, Justus.'

Some of the twelve starting gates shuddered, as though they'd been kicked sharply from inside. The stadium began to seethe and a small boy alongside me begged to be lifted on to his father's shoulders. Everyone's eyes were on the imperial box. Caligula was holding out a white cloth, waiting as the chanting increased in intensity. When it reached screaming point, he opened his hand and let the cloth flutter on to the heads of the spectators. The official on the box above the starting gates yanked a lever. With a snapping noise, the tension in the pulley ropes was released, jerking all twelve pins from their latches and the gates sprang open.

IV

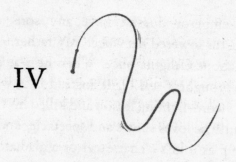

'Come on, the Greens!'

Two hundred thousand voices drowned my cry. Forty-eight horses burst into the arena in a ragged line, twelve charioteers steering their teams of four with their left hand, their whips held in their right. The trailing ends of their reins were wound several times around their waists, giving them more control over the horses' mouths. As they crossed the chalk line that marked the break point where they could leave their start lane, one of the Red charioteers edged into the lead.

'Who's in this race for us?' Justus shouted in my ear.

'Darius, his brother Scylax, and Fuscus.'

'Any good?'

'Darius and Scylax are both brutes, but they're good charioteers. Fuscus isn't – your uncle really should get rid of him. But he's driving Nessus so we want him to do well.'

The lead chariots were approaching the bronze turning posts at the far end of the channel. The Reds' lead driver took the sharp corner neatly, Darius and Scylax shadowing him close behind. Nessus and the three greys outside him were fighting for their heads and as Fuscus took the turn, they swung very wide and almost collided with the second Red chariot.

'Look at Papa.' I pointed below, to the pits at the edge of the track where trainers from each faction were waving their arms and shouting instructions to their teams. 'He's telling Fuscus to shorten his reins, I'll bet you. You've got to hug the turn, don't leave room for anyone to overtake you on the inside.'

The end of the first lap was signalled by the release of a gold dolphin. The Red driver held the lead from Darius and Scylax, with the rest of the pack strung out behind. Rocks and tablets scrawled with violent curses were being flung on to the track from sections of the crowd, aimed at charioteers from rival factions. Fabius and the Four Winds were cantering easily at the back of the field.

'He doesn't seem to be going very fast,' said Justus.

'He's playing with them. You wait.'

Two more laps unfolded with little change in positions. On the fourth, the noise from our supporters increased. Darius was whipping up his horses and to my surprise, he managed to pass the Red driver on the straight to take the lead.

'Good overtaking! I didn't know those bays had the speed, to be honest.'

Things got ugly on the fourth lap. A Blue chariot retired with a broken axle and a collision between Scylax and one of the White teams destroyed both chariots and sent debris flying across the track.

'Is that allowed?' asked Justus.

'It's part of the race,' I told him. 'There are umpires, but they're really there to make sure that everyone keeps to their lane before the break and that no one's trying to throw the race.'

'How would they do that?'

'Holding their horses back, deliberately trying to lose if someone's bribed them. Look – Papa is furious with Scylax. The problem with trying to shipwreck someone is you risk getting your own chariot smashed too.'

A roar went up from the other side of the Circus where most of the Blues' supporters were gathered. I looked back down the field. Fabius had raised his whip hand.

'Here he goes!' I grabbed Justus's arm. 'Watch this!'

The Four Winds' heads all came up together and

their pace suddenly quickened. In a single circuit of the track, they overtook six teams. The Red driver who was still in second glanced warily over his shoulder. Fabius veered to the right and his opponent moved as well, to stop him overtaking. But with an incredible burst of speed, the Four Winds changed direction. I could have sworn Boreas grinned at the Red team's inside horse as they sped past on the left. Fabius waved his whip in salute and the Blues' supporters stood as one to applaud.

'He's a bit arrogant,' shouted Justus.

'He can afford to be,' I yelled back.

Two laps to go. Darius held the lead, but Fabius was fast closing on him. As they came to the turn, Darius misjudged his approach, clipping the wall of the channel. The chariot swerved, almost throwing him from the basket. The mistake cost him. The Four Winds lengthened their stride once more, and it was obvious that for the first time in the race, they were being allowed to show off their true speed. Their necks stretched, their nostrils widened. Within moments, they had left Darius's horses in their wake. I couldn't stop myself from standing up and cheering with the Blues' supporters in the stadium.

'You'd better hope my uncle doesn't see you,' said Justus, laughing.

The sixth dolphin dropped its nose. There was one more lap to go. Darius glanced behind him again and relaxed his hands on the reins, clearly content to settle for second place. I looked back down the field to see what was happening.

'Fuscus has got a chance of third! Come on, Fuscus! No, don't attack him on the bend, you'll never have the pace, wait until you're in the straight again!'

But to my amazement, Nessus and his grey companions nipped past the Red chariot with room to spare. They tore towards the finish and now it was the turn of every Green supporter in the stadium to cheer.

'He's going to do it, he's going to do it, he's done it!' I started jumping up and down even before Fuscus had crossed the line. 'Nessus, you beauty! That's a second *and* a third place, Papa's going to be so pleased...'

I paused mid-celebration, noticing that the grey coats of Nessus and his team were dappled with foam. Despite crossing the finishing line, they hadn't slowed. In fact, they were going faster, their galloping legs flailing like a tangle of spiders. Spittle sprayed from their mouths and their eyes bulged from their heads. They flew past Fabius, who was cantering on his victory lap, and still they kept going.

'Pull them up, why doesn't he pull them up?' asked Justus.

'I don't think he can. Something's wrong.'

Fuscus was leaning back against the reins now, trying to use the weight of his whole body to slow his team down. Someone behind us shouted a warning and I saw the uncleared debris on the track from an earlier collision. Too late, Fuscus saw it. His chariot bounced and with an eruption of splintering wood, the axle disintegrated under his feet. Trapped by the long reins wound around his waist, he jerked forward and was dragged along the floor of the Circus.

Some of the crowd started to cheer but their taunts were smothered by the Green supporters yelling urgently.

'Get your knife, Fuscus!' I shouted. 'Cut the reins!'

I could see him grabbing wildly for his knife in the pocket of his leather corselet. They practised for this, of course. I'd seen Antonius demonstrating the technique to the drivers. *Grab the knife as if you're going to stab someone*, he would say, *then slice. Don't change your grip and be quick, your life might depend on it.* But Nessus and the other greys were hurtling so fast, terrified of the strange burden chasing them along the sand, and Fuscus couldn't free the dagger from beneath his twisting body. One of his leg protectors was torn off, leaving his skin exposed. I closed my eyes. When I was little, I had seen the body of a charioteer who had died like this, strips of skin peeling from his raw flesh, his body like a broken doll. The image had given me nightmares ever since. Somewhere nearby, someone was laughing, a wail of enjoyment that made me shiver.

I opened my eyes and saw Antonius, climbing out of the pit on to the track. Somehow he leaped on Nessus's back as the greys tried to dodge him. Reaching with both hands, he grabbed the reins either side of the bit and eventually dragged the whole team to a skidding halt. Stewards ran towards Fuscus with a stretcher. The shouting of the crowd subsided, and I unclenched my fists. I could hear Justus exhaling.

'He's all right. He's all right, he's moving his head. I thought he was a dead man for certain.'

But I wasn't looking at Fuscus. I'd suddenly realised where the laughter was coming from. Caligula was on his feet, doubled over and shaking with enjoyment, seemingly oblivious to the puzzled stares from the spectators around him.

V

Porcellus's ears twitched. I moved slowly.

'Easy, Porcellus. Easy.'

I finished buckling the straps that secured the girth to the yoke above his withers. Porcellus's ears continued to flick back and forth but he stayed still long enough for me to step up on to the springs of the chariot and hold the reins. Encouraged, I put one foot in front of the other and braced my knee against the low semi-circular guard.

'Walk on.'

Porcellus leaped straight into a canter, so that I almost overbalanced. I heard a belch of drunken laughter. Darius and Scylax were leaning over the railing of the Greens' club-house balcony, watching me.

'Stop embarrassing me,' I hissed at Porcellus, hauling myself upright and tugging on the reins.

He flicked his tail playfully but to my relief, he obeyed my command and quickly settled into a spirited trot. We did a few circles of the small practice arena so that I could concentrate on trying to keep his stride even. Then, the real test. I pointed him towards the line of eight wooden posts that were used by the charioteers to practise their turns. *This time*, I thought to myself. *This time we're going to do it*. Keeping the reins as short as I could, I steered Porcellus round the first post, then the second, weaving in and out along the line. He was light and quick on his feet, like a deer-hound following a scent.

'Yes, come on, almost there... oh...'

I swore as the back wheel clouted the sixth post. There was another cheer from the club-house balcony.

'You need to prepare for the next turn sooner, Dido.'

Antonius was leaning against the fence, watching us with a smile as an orange sun set over the club-house behind him.

'Well, you show me, then.'

A few moments later, we were approaching the posts, Antonius balanced on the back edge of the chariot. He tapped my hand to get me to shorten my rein a little but otherwise he didn't interfere.

'Bend your knees more, keep them soft... concentrate on one turn at a time... but then look ahead to the next straightaway… that's it… that's it… harder on the inside rein… don't let him bully you…'

On the third pass, much to my delight, we managed to negotiate the posts without hitting a single one.

'Don't you think he's come on, Papa?'

'I have to admit, I'm impressed.'

'He's going to be so brilliant. He needs someone better than me to bring him on, really.'

'I don't know, Dido. I think you're doing a pretty good job. He trusts you, and trust is important with a horse like this.'

He let me do another run by myself then called me in and walked beside me as I drove Porcellus slowly back towards the stables next to the club-house. Darius and Scylax had disappeared from the balcony.

'How's Fuscus?' I asked.

'He'll live. A broken rib or two, some bad grazing from the Circus floor. He's lucky it wasn't worse.'

'Fabius would never have let a team get away from him like that.'

'You do know he drives for the Blues?' teased Antonius.

'I know. But he *is* the greatest, isn't he?'

'Maybe. Maybe not.'

'Who's the best charioteer you've ever seen?'

'The best charioteer I've ever seen...' Antonius deliberated for a while, '... was a man by the name of Scorpus. Scorpus of the Blues.'

'Who? I've never even heard of him.'

'I'm not surprised. He only raced at the Circus for a few months.'

'What happened? Did he die?'

'No. He left Rome and never came back. Became a trainer, set up a stable in Africa. Otho buys some of his horses off him, so I've heard.'

'And why was he so good?'

'Some drivers are pure racers. Scorpus had more natural talent than anyone I'd ever seen, before or since.'

'What, even Fabius? I don't believe you.'

'Fabius is good. But believe me, Scorpus had instincts Fabius won't ever have. He was completely ruthless. Second place was of no interest to him. It was winning or nothing. He raced without fear, something I could never do.'

'Did you ever beat him?'

'A few times. But only when I had the very best horses. Scorpus could beat people even when they were driving better teams than him. That's the true test of a great charioteer.'

'So, what happened? Why did he stop racing?'

We had reached the stables and Antonius was unhitching Porcellus from the chariot. He hadn't answered my question and I thought maybe he didn't hear me.

'Why did he stop?' I repeated.

'He lost the taste for it, I suppose.'

I shook my head, unable to understand this.

'How could anyone get tired of racing at the Circus Maximus? I'd do anything to be allowed to do it, even once.'

'Sometimes you lose the hunger. A bad crash can do it to you, all kinds of reasons.'

'Were you friends with him?'

'No.'

'Why not?'

There was a closed look on Antonius's face that surprised me, as if he regretted starting the conversation.

'It's not easy being friends with your competitors.'

I was pondering this when I heard footsteps.

'I'm sorry to interrupt,' said Justus, sounding out of breath. 'It's just that I wondered if… I wanted to show Dido something. It won't take long, but if she's busy…'

I looked pleadingly at Antonius. He smiled.

'Go on then. I'll stable Porcellus. Don't be out too late though, Dido.'

VI

'Do you see it?' whispered Justus.

We were standing under a fig tree in Ruga's private garden. I looked up to see what Justus was pointing at. Indigo clouds were rolling across the lavender sky. Behind us, the sound of laughter and music drifted from the open windows of the club-house.

'I can't even tell what we're looking at.'

'There. *There*. Look! Do you see it? A *green* bird. Where do you think it's come from?'

As soon as I had managed to stop laughing, I explained.

'It's not *really* green. There's an old man down by the Circus who sells tunics and things, you know – different colours for the different factions. He brings cages of birds with him and after every race, he releases a bird coloured to match the faction that's won. How funny that the bird should have known the right club-house to come to.'

'How does he make them change colour?'

'Dips them in the dye he uses for the clothes. Poor birds. It can't be good for them.'

Since it was not yet dark, we decided to head out of the side gate and take a stroll through the porticoes and narrow streets surrounding the club-house. The four factions dominated this quarter of the city and the taverns along Stable Street were full of grooms and stable hands, their drinking games and dice matches spilling over the thresholds. The smell of sour wine wafted out of open doorways, and snack vendors did a steady trade, thanks to the faction supporters milling around, hoping to run into one of their racing heroes. I looked over at Justus, feeling shy and stupid all of a sudden as I searched for something to say.

'So what have you made of it? Your first month in Rome?'

'Different from the countryside.' Justus laughed and pushed a hand through his hair. 'It's been exciting though. I enjoy the races and being near the horses, much more than I thought. I wish I could have talked to my father about it. He didn't really approve of chariot-racing.'

'How could anyone not approve of chariot-racing? What's so—' I stopped, worried that it sounded as though I was being rude.

'I'm not sure, if I'm honest. I think he thought it brought out the worst in people. You know – caring so much about whichever faction wins that they'll start a fight over it. He's gone now though, so I suppose I'll have to decide what I think for myself. I miss talking to him.'

He hesitated. I somehow sensed what he was going to ask.

'Dido? Do you mind if I ask you what happened to your mother? Don't tell me if you don't want to.'

I smiled. He looked so awkward and sweet.

'No, I don't mind. I like talking about her. She came from a place called Thugga, on the other side of the sea. Papa says my grandfather Muttumbaal was a great racehorse trainer, and so my mother grew up with horses, just like me. She ran away to Rome when she was fifteen and joined a group of acrobats who did riding tricks to entertain the crowd between races at the Circus. That's how she met Papa. They fell in love and had me. Then one day, a trick she was doing went wrong in the arena, and…' I shrugged, running my fingers lightly against the wall alongside us.

'Do you remember her at all?'

'No. I wasn't even a year old when she died. She had dark curly hair, I know that. Papa keeps a lock of it in a little box. He says I look like her. Except for my eyes and my hair. I got those from him.' I pulled out the chain from under the neck of my tunic and showed him the silver crescent dangling from it. 'This was hers. Papa bought it for her out of his winnings from a big race. She always wore it. That's a little "S" scratched on it, see? For her name, Sophonisba.'

We'd reached the main entrance to the Green club-house.

'Well. I'd better go back to the stables and help Papa. I suppose you'll be going to the party?'

Justus nodded.

'Uncle Ruga did say I should be there. He wants to introduce me to some people, other investors in the faction, that kind of thing. I wish I didn't have to, though. I'd much rather stay out here with you.'

I felt my cheeks getting warm and pretended to be retying the twine in my hair.

'Oh, well. You'll see me tomorrow.'

'That's true. I'll be up bright and early, I promise. Ready for another day of torture.'

'You think today was torture? Tomorrow, I'm going to teach you about mucking out the stalls.'

'Excellent. I'm sure to be wonderful at it.' He grinned. 'Goodnight, Dido.'

'Goodnight, Justus. Enjoy your party.'

He waved at me as he disappeared into the club-house.

Feeling light-headed and happy, I decided to make a final check of the horses who were in for the night. The stables were behind the club-house, in three long buildings connected by a courtyard. Each horse had its own stall, facing a walkway through which you passed into the next yard. As I reached the second stable block, I saw Porcellus waiting for me, his silky black head poking over the half-door. He whickered as I approached and his nose went immediately to the pouch at my waist.

'Wait, Porcellus, just wait, you're always so impatient. There.'

I held out the special treat I gave him each night, a fig plucked from the trees that grew wild on the Field of Mars. He chewed it with relish as I rubbed his head.

''Night, my beautiful boy. One day that'll be you out there in front of the crowds. You're going to be the greatest horse the Circus Maximus has ever seen. I just know it.'

Usually Porcellus would be in the stall next to Nessus, but Antonius had ordered that he be put out for the night in the Greens' grazing pasture on the northern corner of the Field of Mars. His stall was messy, so I went inside to tidy it. As I picked up some loose hay, I kicked something hard in the straw bedding. A jar rolled out of the open stable door into the walkway, leaving a thin trail of liquid. I picked the jar up and examined it by the light of an oil lamp on the wall. There was something glinting red inside and a warm, bitter scent filled my nostrils. I shook the jar and a berry fell out. It looked like it came from a yew tree, which I knew very well was poisonous to horses.

I headed for our sleeping quarters directly above Porcellus's stable block, assuming I'd find Antonius there. But there was a lamp light in the harness room. There I found both Antonius and Atticus, having a drink. Atticus was half-slumped over the table.

'What is it, Dido?'

I showed my father the little red fruit.

'I found this in Nessus's stable. It looks like it could be yew. Do you think someone tried to poison him?'

Antonius examined the berry in the middle of his palm, deep lines appearing in his brow. 'This isn't yew,' he said.

'What is it then?'

He stood up, the legs of his chair scraping the floor.

'Where are you going?' slurred Atticus.

'To talk to Ruga.'

'Oh, leave it alone, Antonius. Honestly, it was only a few races, where's the harm...'

Antonius stopped in the doorway. He turned and stared at his friend. I looked at Atticus and saw he had shifted his feet under the table. Suddenly he wouldn't meet my father's eye.

'Go to bed, Dido.' The tone of Antonius's voice frightened me.

'But...'

'I said, go to bed. Atticus and I need to talk.'

VII

I woke up feeling cold. How long had I been lying here? The oil lamp had burned itself out, but I could see by the light of the moon on his empty straw pallet that Antonius wasn't back.

Our room had almost no furniture, just our two mattresses and the wooden chest where we stored a few clothes and possessions. There was a drawer in the chest which I wasn't supposed to open but sometimes I did when Antonius wasn't about. Wondering where he was and why he had seemed so angry with Atticus, I tugged at the drawer handle and breathed in the smell of lavender which kept the moths out. I picked up the little box and lifted its delicate clay lid. Gently, I touched the curl of brown hair inside before putting it back. The box sat on top of a carefully folded white tunic, trimmed on the sleeves and hem with gold thread that was frayed and tangled. Antonius told me that my mother used to have to restitch the thread every time she wore the costume for a performance. I wanted to look at it but I didn't trust myself to fold the tunic neatly enough so that Antonius wouldn't know I'd been in there. I closed the drawer and as I did, I heard raised voices in the yard below.

I clambered down the ladder that led from our quarters. Keeping to the shadows, I peered round the corner. Three figures were standing in a pool of light cast by a lamp at the entrance to the stable block. One was Antonius. I could tell straightaway from the way he was standing with his hands on his hips that he was furious. The second was Atticus, his arms folded like a child caught making mischief. The third was Ruga, whose face I couldn't see, but who was jabbing his finger in my father's face.

'Don't presume to dictate to me, Antonius.' His words cut through the crisp night air. 'You think the faction followers give a damn about your scruples? You think it counts as a fair fight when the Blues are funded by a man with more money than me and the other faction leaders put together? Maybe you don't mind if Otho keeps winning. Maybe you need to decide where your loyalty lies.'

'I need your word, Ruga.' My father was a head shorter than his faction master but he was looking at him as though they were equals. 'That we won't ever win this way again. How can I look my daughter in the eye and tell her that her father's reputation as a trainer is based on a lie? That he cheated his way to victory? Frankly, I'd rather never win another race if that's the price I have to pay.'

As the current of their angry words continued to ebb and flow, something on the other side of the yard caught my eye. A sliver of white peeled out of the inky gloom and the hairs on the back of my neck stood up. But the figure that entered the glowing halo of the lamp was not a ghost, as I had first feared. It was Macro, the man I had seen with Ruga outside the Circus. His thick arms swung by his sides, as though he was out for an evening stroll. Antonius and Ruga had seen him too and fell silent.

Macro stopped in front of them and nodded.

'Everything all right, gentlemen?'

Ruga muttered something I couldn't hear.

'Didn't seem like that to me,' came Macro's reply.

'I said, I'm handling it.' Ruga sounded panicked.

I saw Macro move his arm, as though he was shaking out the folds of his cloak. I thought he was turning to leave. Instead he punched my father hard in the stomach.

'No!'

I stepped from the shadows. Another shout had muffled my voice and none of them turned. Atticus charged forward to catch Antonius just as his knees buckled. Ruga stepped back and now I could see his face too and the expression of shock on it. I waited for Atticus to help my father to his feet. Then I saw the knife buried to its hilt in the front of my father's tunic. There was a dark stain spreading around it. My hand went to my own belly, as though the wound was mine.

'No, no... Antonius... come on, my old friend.' Atticus was cradling my father in his arms, like a parent rocking a sick child full of the shivers to sleep. 'We're not done yet. Plenty of winners still left in you. Come on. I'm sorry. I'm so, so sorry...'

Antonius turned his head, as though the light above him was too bright. He looked straight at me. A strange sound throbbed in my ears. I could see his lips moving and I realised what he was trying to say.

Dido. Dido.

His eyes held mine and I could feel the connection between us. For a precious, desperate moment, I clung to it. Then the thread broke, and I felt a wave of something so unbearable, so impossible to understand, that I thought I might fall. The only sound was Atticus sobbing.

'The girl. She found it. Isn't that what you said?' Macro was looking at me, scratching his bristled chin in the same way our race engineer did when he was trying to decide how best to mend a broken chariot. Ruga, who seemed rooted to the spot, shook his head.

'No. Do you hear me, Macro? I said, no.'

Macro continued to look at me in that thoughtful way. Then he spoke again, quietly and bluntly.

'Can't be helped. Pity. But she might start rumours.'

He began to walk towards me like a groom might approach a tricky horse he was trying to catch, glancing to his right at the archway that led through the stable block to the next yard. I knew he was assessing the distance between the archway and my position, calculating how quickly he needed to act. Ruga called out. I understood the danger, but my legs wouldn't move. It was as if I was in a dream and someone was shouting at me to wake up, but I couldn't.

Atticus sprang from the ground. Like a bull, he charged at Macro, bringing him crashing down. The two men started to struggle.

'Run, Dido! Run!'

VIII

I wasn't sure if it was Ruga or Atticus shouting at me. But the feeling returned to my legs and I started running. One of the two brawling shapes got up and kicked the other's head. I didn't see any more because I was through the archway, flying down the walkway between the stalls, into the next yard and then charging through the door set into the heavy wooden gate that led on to Stable Street.

The door swung shut. I was in the middle of a crowd of Green faction followers. Loud music and laughter were coming from the windows of the club-house above our heads. The door handle turned behind me. I plunged into the crowd, swerving to avoid drunken pedestrians. Shouts rang out but I didn't look back as I tore down the street. Pale faces loomed from the darkness, like meddling spirits. A pair of drinkers in the doorway of a tavern shouted encouragement as I sped past. I looked back. The white of a praetorian uniform was threading in and out of the crowd, moving fast.

I turned down a side street. There was a bakery where Antonius bought me pancakes as a treat sometimes. The owner knew me well. But when I reached it, the bars were across the doors and there was no lamp lit inside. I turned left, then right, heading deeper and deeper into a part of the city I didn't know. I had no shoes on and my bare feet kept slipping in puddles of water and filth. It was painful to breathe, but I didn't dare stop running.

I turned another corner. An avenue stretched ahead, lined with billowing cloths like a fleet of sails. It was a street of fullers' shops and the cloths were drying laundry, spread across washing lines hung from building to building. Trying to tread lightly and not disturb the long strips of linen as I brushed past, I weaved my way through. About half-way down the alley, I paused and listened. All I could hear was water dripping. But somehow I sensed that I wasn't alone. Someone else was listening, as hard as I was. Then I heard it again, way down the alley, but distinct and closer now. *Splash, splash.*

I started to run. There was a strong breeze blowing from the other end of the street, catching the edges of the heavy cloths which smelled faintly of the urine in which they'd been washed. I pushed past the last one and suddenly I knew where I was. I had reached the bank of the river Tiber, where ships brought in supplies for the stables and other businesses in this quarter of the city. A row of ships was moored to the quayside, and men were traipsing on and off with crates and barrels.

Among the vessels was a small deep-hulled animal transport with no crew on board that I could see. I ran as quickly as I could, jumping from street level and collapsing on to the ship's deck. My eyes fell on a dirty sailcloth and I dived underneath it, my heart hammering in my chest. Had I been fast enough? I tweaked the edge of the cloth so that I could peer out. No sign of anyone. Then something thudded on the deck beside my head and I ducked under the cloth again. Someone very close by spoke.

'What is it, Mathos?'

'Thought I heard something up on deck.'

'Can you see anything?'

Mathos swore quietly.

'Praetorians. Look, over there. They're searching the boats. Some idiot told on us. Rufus, take the steering oar, get us out into the current. Abascantus, cast off, as quietly as you can.'

Feet padded around me. The boat tilted suddenly, and I could hear water slapping against the hull. The deck was rising and falling.

'Have they seen us?'

'Don't think so. Get behind that barge there, give us some cover.'

Someone stifled a laugh.

'That was close. Too close.'

'You're telling me. Odd, though. It's not like the Praetorian Guard to take an interest in a bit of harmless back-street wine trade.'

'One of these days they're going to catch us, Mathos.'

'Don't be such a chicken-heart, Rufus. Race days are when we make our best money. That's good, the current's strong, we're well away now. Without a cargo we should make it back to Carthage inside four days if we catch a good wind out of Ostia.'

Blood was pounding in my ears. I prayed for Papa to shake me awake from the nightmare I was trapped in. But the rough planks under my palms and the damp breeze pinching at the sailcloth were horribly real. My father's green eyes pierced the darkness. I saw fear and pain in them, and I ground my forehead into the deck, feeling a numbing emptiness seeping through me. He couldn't be gone. He couldn't be.

The crescent moon of my mother's necklace tickled my chin. A memory came to me, like a single star glinting in a black sky. *Carthage*. That's where those sailors had said they were heading. I used to beg Antonius to tell me the story of how my mother ran away from home. Her father, Muttumbaal, had wanted her to get married and she didn't like the man he had chosen for her. So she hid herself in a grain wagon from Thugga to Carthage and had taken a boat from there to Rome. Was it possible my grandfather still lived at Thugga? Would he help me, in spite of how Mama had disobeyed him?

'Right, we've got the wind behind us now. Abascantus, get that sail up.'

I didn't have time to think. The damp weight of the sailcloth suddenly lifted. A small bearded man peered down at me.

'What the...! Here, Mathos, Rufus, there's a *girl* on board.'

Two more heads appeared. One belonged to a man with flint-coloured eyes and a grey, stubbled chin. The other was that of a younger man with thick reddish-brown hair and freckled skin.

'Where did she come from?' he asked.

'Knew I'd heard something on deck,' said the older sailor. 'Probably some street kid, looking for a chance to steal our cargo.'

'No, no, wait, please.' I scrambled to my feet, slipping on the wet deck. 'Please help me. Someone was trying to kill me. I didn't know where else to hide.'

'That doesn't recommend you. Go on.' He pointed to the side of the boat. 'Start swimming.'

'She's just a kid, Mathos,' said the red-haired sailor.

'You're a soft touch, Rufus. A bit of cold water won't hurt her.' His eyes narrowed in suspicion. 'Hang on. It wasn't you the Praetorians were after back there, was it?'

I hesitated.

'Even if it was, Mathos, what do we care? It's not as if the Praetorians are friends of ours,' said Rufus.

'True. But we don't need any trouble. All the more reason to ditch her.'

'Did you say you were going to Carthage?' I asked. 'Will you take me with you?'

'You've got some cheek, girl. This isn't a passenger service. Don't suppose you can even pay your way, can you?'

I hesitated.

'Here.' I fumbled with the knot at the back of my neck. I hated having to give up my mother's charm. But I was sure she had spoken to me somehow a moment ago and perhaps this was her idea too, to help me reach my grandfather.

Mathos held up the necklace, inspecting the crescent moon.

'Solid silver,' he said. 'What's a grubby kid like you doing with an expensive trinket like this?'

'It was my mother's. My father gave it to her. She came from Thugga. If I can get there, I might be able to find her family.'

'Come on, Mathos,' said Rufus. 'What trouble is it to us? We can get her as far as Carthage at least. No need to take what little she has from her.'

Mathos seemed to be having a silent argument with himself. Then he grunted and threw the chain back to me.

'Fine. Keep your necklace. We had a good night tonight and I'm in a generous mood. We'll get you to Carthage but then you're on your own.'

IX

Somewhere in the distance, I could hear a horse neighing.

'Porcellus?'

I opened my eyes. The sky overhead was a cloudless blue. I realised that for the first time since we'd left port at Ostia the horizon was steady. Sitting up, I saw that we were in a huge, circular harbour, moored in the middle of a row of other ships. Sunshine poured down on the deck. Rufus was cooking something in a pot. He smiled at me and waved his wooden spoon.

'Want some breakfast?'

The smell was tempting. I'd barely been able to eat anything during the crossing; I kept throwing it back up again. I'd made plenty of sea voyages with Antonius but never in such a small boat or through water licked into rough peaks by early autumn winds. Rufus had made a bed of blankets for me in the cargo hold but it reeked of stale animal dung down there and after a while I'd decided it was better sleeping in the open air, even if that meant being bitterly cold. Staggering across the slippery deck, I took the bowl Rufus was offering and wolfed the warm porridge, scooping it out with my fingers.

'Why can I hear horses?' I asked through a mouthful.

'Up there.' Rufus pointed with his spoon towards a vast citadel towering over the harbour. 'Carthage. Greatest market in the empire. Best racehorses come from here too.'

I accepted another spoonful of porridge from him, wondering why Antonius hadn't ever come here to buy new horses for Ruga, if Carthage was such a good place to get them. Hispania was a much longer journey. Then again, maybe he just liked buying from Marius. Or maybe visiting the place where my mother had come from was too upsetting for him. The image of my father lying dead in Atticus's arms escaped from the place where I had locked it away. I slammed my mind shut.

'Where are Mathos and Abascantus?' I asked.

'They don't like my cooking. They've gone to find something better from the market stalls.'

'Where will you go after this?'

'We do this run between Carthage and Rome every

month or so. Sometimes with horses, sometimes with beasts for the shows at the Circus. We're a small crew so we only take a few animals at a time. They make good wine here as well as good horses, so we sneak it through Ostia and avoid the port duties. Keeps us in profit,' he added with a wink.

I wiped the bowl clean with my fingers and handed it back.

'Thank you,' I said. 'And thank you for taking me with you.'

He felt inside the pouch at his belt and took out a couple of silver coins, which he gave to me.

'These might come in useful later if you get hungry. Head up the hill there, turn left at the big temple, and follow your ears and your nose – you'll get to the market. Maybe you'll find someone there who knows this grandfather of yours and can get you to Thugga. It's only a day or two's journey from here.' He gave me a little salute. 'Good luck, Dido. You're better company than I'm used to having at sea. Stay safe out there.'

It felt for a moment as though he might be the only friend I had. I wanted to ask if I might stay with him. I had learned how to manage a horse as well as any boy. Maybe I could do the same with a boat. But I knew what the answer would be. I said goodbye and joined the throng of people and animals making their way from the harbour towards the citadel.

It was a steep climb and my legs were shaky from the sea voyage. Carthage felt both like and unlike Rome. There were temples and elegant flat-roofed houses and shop fronts with apartments on the floors above. But many in the jostling crowd spoke a language I didn't understand and there was a different smell in the air. Maybe it was the breeze coming off the sea or maybe it was the cauldrons on the counters of the cook shops which bubbled with strange stews. A group of women washing clothes on some steps looked at me as I went past. One said something which made the others laugh and I realised how dirty I must look. My bare feet were still coated in the filth of Rome's streets.

Finally, the steep road curved to the left beside a large temple, just as Rufus had said it would, and then opened into a vast marketplace, seething with people. I kept to the edge, listening to the jabber of different tongues, looking at the various stalls. Everything appeared to be for sale, from olive oil, wine and spices, to oxen, mules and people. A line of horribly thin slaves, chained at the ankle, huddled against a wall. A dealer shouted out their prices. There was a little girl among them, with hollow cheeks and straggly hair. She gazed at me from inside the fold of a slave-woman's dress, her tired eyes dull and empty.

I reached the far side of the marketplace. Something lifted inside me. Wherever I looked there were horses of every colour, size and breed. Some were tied up with their noses in feed troughs, others were being walked up and down in front of men standing in pairs and small groups who watched and conferred intently. A few of the animals were packhorses for pulling carts, but most were clearly racing breeds, small and well-muscled, built for speed and stamina. Alongside the horses were stalls trading in chariots and harness. One was selling tunics in the colours of the four factions of Rome. Crowds of children lingered, watched closely by the stallholder who barked if they came too close. I saw several boys wearing faded green tunics, just like mine. What would they say if I was to tell them that I worked in the Green stables, that I was on speaking terms with their heroes and had groomed their favourite horses? I thought of Porcellus, with his soft black coat and the white star between his brilliant brown eyes. Was he wondering where I was and why I hadn't brought him his evening fig for the last four nights?

Blinking away tears, I tried to distract myself by searching the crowd for a friendly face. Two men were surveying a line of horses. The larger of them wore a long tunic and a patchwork cap, and was talking and gesturing with his whip to a groom trotting a chestnut horse in front of them. I approached.

'Could you help me, please?'

The man in the cap waved his whip irritably.

'Not now. We're doing business here.' He leaned towards his companion, a slim, brown-skinned man who was studying the chestnut's gait with crossed arms and a frown. 'Look at that knee lift. That's the Libyan in her, you never find that in one of your Spanish breeds...'

'Please. I'm looking for someone who might know my grandfather. He's from Thugga and his name's—'

'I told you, we're busy,' spat the dealer. 'Get lost.'

He flicked his whip, catching me with the tail of it. Feeling despondent, I went to look at the horses for sale. They were mostly African breeds, Libyans and Mauretanians, a few Sicilians as well. A blue roan with beautiful eyes half-hidden by his untrimmed forelock caught my eye. He had a neat, intelligent head and white speckles in his dark grey coat. I couldn't help running a hand along his spine and down his legs to his hooves, checking for soundness as Antonius had taught me. Stroking the roan's warm muzzle as he blinked peaceably made me feel calm and safe again. Then my head jerked back as someone grabbed me by the hair.

'Get your hands off that animal.'

I banged my head as I was pushed to the ground. The dealer stood over me menacingly, his whip raised.

'You stay away from my horses. You hear me, you little brat?'

'Wait, Gisco.' The dealer's customer held him by the wrist. 'Leave her be.'

I looked up into the man's hard, bright eyes. His stubbled chin was flecked with grey, but he had smooth, unlined skin. Seeing his hand reaching down to my throat, I shrank away. He took hold of the little silver crescent on its chain which had escaped from inside my tunic and examined it by the light of the sun.

'Where did you get this?'

'My father gave it to me.'

'What's your father's name?'

'Antonius.' I saw something flicker in the man's eyes.

'Is he here?'

'No. He's...'

I couldn't say the words. The silver chain fell back against my neck. There was something odd about the expression on the man's face. I felt certain that he knew Antonius somehow. It was a thread of connection and I clung to it.

'Are you thinking of buying that horse?' I pointed to the chestnut being walked up and down in the distance.

'Not sure yet.'

'Don't. His hooves are weak. They've been oiled to make them look stronger, but they'll never last beyond a couple of seasons.'

Gisco raised his whip again.

'Why, you little...'

I scrambled to my feet and leaped out of range.

'If it's for the Circus you're looking, then this one's much better.' I took refuge behind the roan. 'He'll make a rope horse, I think. See? He's got strong forelegs, nice balance in the shoulders, and you can tell he'd train well – see how alert he is.'

The man picked up the card tied to the roan's mane. 'Icarus,' he read aloud. 'Two years old. Gaetulian sire, Libyan dam.'

'It's not such a good horse as the chestnut,' said Gisco defensively.

'Maybe. It's certainly not as expensive.' The man was kneeling now, feeling the roan's legs. 'But she's right about the hooves, I spotted it the moment you had him walked out. That trick has never worked on me, Gisco.'

Gisco scowled.

Why are you listening to this little girl? You want that chestnut or not? I've got other buyers, Scorpus, don't keep me waiting all day.'

My heart leaped.

'Scorpus of the Blues?' I asked.

The man straightened up and looked at me.

'You know me?'

'Yes. My father told me about you. You used to race against each other at the Circus. You're a trainer now.' Excitement was making my words come out in a rush. 'Can you help me? Please, I don't know anyone else here.'

Scorpus continued to look at me strangely. Then he turned to Gisco, who was slapping his whip angrily against his leg.

'I'll leave the chestnut. How much for the roan?'

X

Were you friends?
  No.
Why not?
It's not easy being friends with your competitors.
  I glanced sideways at Scorpus, who was squinting into the sun. The only attention he'd paid me during the whole journey was to pass me a water sack from time to time. The feeling I'd had in the marketplace of a faint understanding between us had gone. I couldn't tell whether he was angry or bored by my company, and was left to stare through the open sides of the wagon at the rolling green landscape on one side and the endless blue sea on the other, wondering where we were going.

  As the sun climbed to the sky's peak, we stopped to rest in the shade of some trees. When Scorpus offered me half a pastry, I grabbed it and started stuffing it into my mouth. It was filled with meat and spices, crumbly and good. I wondered if his wife had made it.

'Your name's Dido. That right?' Scorpus grunted, once we had settled into some cool grass under a tree. My cheeks were full, so I nodded in reply.

'Named for a queen of Carthage.'

'I know. Papa told me.'

'That's a lot to live up to.' He waited for me to finish my mouthful.

'What happened to your father?'

I picked some of the crust off the pastry, watching as the insects in the grass swarmed over it. How much should I tell him? I no longer trusted him as I had an hour or so ago in the marketplace. He and Antonius had been great rivals after all. What if Scorpus decided to take revenge on him by sending me back to Rome, back to Macro?

'There was an accident… in training.'

'I see. Couldn't you have stayed in Rome? Someone must have been able to look after you.'

'No. It's always just been me and Papa.'

'How did you get here?'

'I hid on a boat. Papa told me my grandfather lived in Thugga. I thought I might be able to find him. His name's Muttumbaal, he's a trainer, like you. Do you know him?'

'I did. But it won't do you any good.'

'What do you mean?'

Scorpus paused and didn't quite meet my eye.

'He's dead. Passed away a few years ago.'

It was hard to feel grief for a relative I had never met. But Scorpus's words were like a drench of cold water all the same. I felt even lonelier in the world than I had been.

'Where are we going now?' I asked.

'Looks like you're going to have to stay with me for a while. Not as though you've got any other options, is it?'

I thought about this and decided he was probably right. Stealing another look at his unsmiling face, I wondered why he was helping me. The unwelcome thought that I was being kidnapped into slavery had occurred to me. But it was a peculiar person who would share their lunch with a slave.

'Papa said you train horses for the Circus now?'

'I train them. Whether they get to the Circus is up to them.' He finished his pastry and took a swig of water. 'What else did Antonius tell you about me?'

'That you were only with the Blues for a few months, but you were the greatest charioteer he'd ever seen. Then you left and no one ever saw you again or knew why you'd gone.' I looked at him, hoping for an explanation. But he didn't say anything. Silence separated us again.

'How did you know?' I asked.

'How did I know what?'

'Back there in the market. How did you know who I was?'

Scorpus took a bite out of an apple before he answered.

'Your necklace. Antonius used to wear it on his wrist during races. We all had our good luck charms. Made us feel someone was watching over us.'

I touched the crescent of silver on its chain and remembered the feeling I'd had on the boat, as if I was being looked after and shown what to do. 'Papa always said this was my mother's.'

'Then I suppose that's why it was lucky for him.'

He didn't seem interested either in asking or answering anything else. As the heat of the afternoon eased, we climbed into the wagon once more and drove on.

We passed over a wooden bridge crossing a shallow river. In the distance ahead, I could make out the sprawl of a city. 'Utica,' grunted Scorpus, when I asked him its name. Soon we turned off the coast road and headed inland. The warm air smelled of mint and resin and there were pine trees and olive groves, vineyards and lush fields of wheat. A snake slithered out of the way of our wheels. As we drove over the peak of a shallow hill,

I saw a villa built of honey-coloured stone in the valley below. It was surrounded by paddocks full of horses, dozens of them, grazing in rich pasture. There were stables as well as a training arena, and in the distance, an oval practice track. Chariots were circling it like pieces on a gaming board. The wagon rattled down a pebbled path before pulling up in front of the villa. Two young boys of ten or eleven were sitting astride the gate to the stable yard. They wore sleeveless tunics and had lean bodies like deer-hounds. A girl was sweeping the porch. She was about fifteen or sixteen, with smooth brown skin and dark hair in a long plait. She smiled at Scorpus as he climbed down.

'Were you able to find the horses you wanted, Master Scorpus...?'

The question died on her lips as soon as she saw me.

'Hanno, Abibaal, get these mules in.'

The two boys sitting on the gate leaped off and raced each other to be the first to take the reins from Scorpus. Both of them stared curiously at me.

'Who's this, Papa?'

Scorpus ignored them and instead spoke to the girl.

'Anna, this is Dido. Find her a bucket to wash in, clean clothes and something to eat. She'll have to sleep in with you. Did Nicias and Parmenion mend that fence?'

'Yes, Master Scorpus, they say they did.'

He turned to me. There was a coldness in his eyes that surprised me, even frightened me.

'You'll help Anna in the house. You'll do as you're told and count yourself lucky I came along back there. Who knows what could have happened to you. Now, go with Anna. I've done everything that could possibly be expected of me.'

XI

One month later

I woke up suddenly, the sound of splashing footsteps fading from my ears. My body cooled as I listened to Anna's steady breathing on the other side of the mattress. A faint purple light was seeping around the sides of the cloth hung over the high narrow window. I reached under the pillow for my old green tunic which I had refused to let Anna have for washing. Pressing my nose into the warm wool, I breathed in. I didn't know if I was imagining the smell of Porcellus in the smattering of black hairs still clinging to the fabric, but it was comforting all the same. Covering the crumpled garment with the pillow, I quietly dressed in the simple grey tunic Anna had given me.

Our room was next to the kitchen. I took an apple and a jar of honey from the larder shelf, then felt my way along the narrow passage towards the dark atrium of the villa where heavy furniture carved from citrus wood gave off a warm peppery scent. Along the opposite corridor, I listened carefully at the door of Scorpus's room. As I crept away, the door of the room nearest the atrium creaked open and Abibaal's face appeared in the narrow gap.

'I know where you're going,' he whispered.

'Shut up and go back to sleep.'

'Can I come and watch?'

'No.'

'I'll tell Papa what you're doing.'

'And I'll tell Nicias that it was you who took his lucky coin. Go back to bed.'

Outside, the sky glowed amber on the horizon, darkening to the colour of ink at its crown. It had rained in the night and the long, wet grass brushed the bare tops of my feet as I crossed the pasture. Glancing at the stables, I saw that there were no lamps lit yet. Nicias and the other apprentices were all safely asleep. They'd be up in an hour or so, as soon as Scorpus came and rattled the bell below their sleeping quarters.

Icarus was standing by the gate to the furthest field next to the practice track. As soon as he saw me, his eyes widened and a throaty whicker of pleasure rumbled through his nostrils. While he crunched up the apple, I inspected the chafing around his lips.

Taking the lid off the honey, I began to dab it on the raw pink skin.

'Poor darling. They won't let up on you, will they? It's that horrible bit Scorpus uses. Papa never used curb-bits. He always said you could ruin a horse's mouth that way.'

When I had finished treating him, I went to fetch the light training chariot from the nearby shed. Icarus quivered when he heard the wheels behind him but he didn't try to run off like he used to. I left the brutal curb-bit with its sharp edges – like a wolf's teeth – off the bridle as I put the harness on. We started off with a few circles at one end of the track, first at a walk, then building up to a trot. As usual, Icarus took some time to settle. But once he'd realised he wasn't going to be jabbed in the mouth every time he made a mistake, his stride lengthened and soon he was working at an easy canter, responding well to my commands. Finally, I tested his pace on a loop of the whole track. He didn't quite have Porcellus's speed, but he was just as neat and careful with his turns.

The spreading light over the distant mountains told me it was time to stop. I put the harness away then smeared more honey on Icarus's lip. He poked out his tongue to try to lick it off.

'No, leave it. There, go on, off you go, you've got a rest day while the others are racing at Utica.

So you can think about everything you've learned this morning.'

Swishing his tail, Icarus ambled away to rejoin the only other occupant of the field, a spindle-legged old bay called Sciron who was grazing on the other side of the field and paying me no attention whatsoever. But that was Sciron for you. I'd never known a horse I wasn't able to make friends with before I met him. Oddly enough, Icarus was the only one of his stable-mates he seemed to like, so they were always put out to grass together. I wondered why Scorpus kept Sciron when he was too old to race any more. It didn't seem to me that Scorpus had much affection for the horses he trained and sold.

In the next field were the other novices, young horses like Icarus, only recently broken to harness. Snowy and Iris were dozing peacefully under a tree, swatting their freckled grey hindquarters with their tails. Little brown Perdix was enjoying a vigorous roll in the damp grass. Hannibal and Mago grazed contentedly, the sun catching their yellow coats. I leaned my elbows on the fence and watched them all, feeling a deep ache in my heart for Porcellus. What if none of the grooms could manage him, and Ruga decided he had to be sold? How would I ever find him again? My thoughts turned to Justus. I often wondered what his uncle had told him about Antonius and me. Did he think we had just left in the middle of the night without saying goodbye?

The sound of a twig snapping made my shoulders tighten.

'You idiot, Parmenion. We almost had her.'

Nicias and Parmenion were both half-dressed as usual. There was something competitive about the way they liked showing off their lean muscled chests. Parmenion was grinning sleepily, his light brown hair dishevelled like straw. Nicias was also smiling, but his eyes were narrow and malicious. He was hiding something behind his back. As he held it up, I saw that it was a dead mouse, its body mangled by a predator's claws.

'You nearly got this down your neck.' Nicias swung the bloodied little corpse by the tail. 'What are you doing up this early?'

I didn't answer.

'Probably came to see your boyfriend over there. You're a bit *too* interested in that horse, you know. Maybe I should show this to him. He's so scared of everything, he'd probably squeal like a girl.'

'You leave Icarus alone.'

'Oh, come on, Dido. It's just a joke, we can be friends.' Parmenion winked at me. 'Why don't you come back to the barn with me and be friends?'

'You're disgusting.'

Nicias threw the mouse suddenly and I couldn't stop myself from yelping as it brushed my leg. Parmenion howled with laughter. Nicias smirked in triumph.

'What do you think you're doing?'

Their laughter stopped abruptly. Both Nicias and Parmenion looked wary as Scorpus approached, his eyes hooded from sleep. He looked at the remains of the mouse, and then at the boys.

'You're supposed to be feeding the horses by now, not playing stupid games. Antigonus is up, go and join him. We've got a big day of races ahead and an important customer on the way.'

Parmenion nodded and set off towards the barn, but Nicias lingered.

'Who am I driving today? If there's going to be faction scouts there, I want a good team. You always give the best ones to Antigonus.'

'You'll drive whoever I say you're driving. Now get moving.'

Nicias scowled, but retreated without further argument. Scorpus turned to me.

'You're not supposed to be out here. Go inside, Anna needs your help with breakfast.'

'I don't know anything about making breakfast, I just get in her way. Why can't I help with the horses? I'm a good groom, you should give me a chance—'

He cut across me.

'I'm not going to argue about this again. A girl's place is inside the house. Now hurry up.'

As I walked back by the longest route I could, around the edge of the pasture, I passed a line of tall pines, dark giants holding up their arms against the sun-streaked sky. Swifts and larks swooped to settle on their outstretched branches. A small stone grave marker at the edge of the wood caught my eye. I stopped and crouched to look at it. As if startled, the birds flew from the branches, scattering in different directions with a thudding flurry of wings. I peered into the crevices between the trees.

'Dido! Get inside!' Scorpus was waving at me from the other side of the pasture.

I hurried back to the villa, unable to shake the feeling I'd just had. The feeling that there had been someone in the woods, watching me.

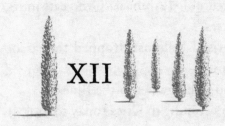

XII

'Come on, Dido!' Hanno shouted from the driving seat. 'We'll be late and Papa will skin us.'

It was almost the middle of the day and the sun was beating down on my back. Anna had insisted that I look smart for Scorpus's important guest and had arranged my hair into a bun with pins that were digging into my head. Stumbling on the hem of my ankle-length tunic, I loaded the last of the baskets on to the back of the wagon. Abibaal came to help.

'How was training?' he whispered with a sly wink.

'Shut up. And you'd better not say a word.'

He hummed annoyingly as he lifted one of the cloths covering the food.

'Smells good, Anna. What is it?'

'Get your nose out of there, it's not for you. You can have some of the leftovers if there are any.'

'Fat chance,' grumbled Abibaal. 'Otho eats more than his own horses.'

I was so surprised I almost dropped the jar of wine I was carrying.

'Opellius Otho? The owner of the Blues?'

'The same. He's coming to Utica today to look at some of our horses.'

Hanno slung himself around in his seat.

'Is it true that your father and Papa used to race each other at the Circus Maximus?'

I nodded as I finally managed to heave the heavy jar on to the wagon.

'Which faction did he drive for?' demanded Abibaal.

'The Greens.'

'So how did they become friends if they weren't on the same team?'

'I don't know if you'd really call them friends.'

Abibaal frowned.

'Then why would Papa invite you to live with us? He said he knew your father, and that he had died and you didn't have anywhere else to go.'

'I think... they respected each other. As competitors.'

Hanno nodded as though this made perfect sense, though I could see Abibaal still looked confused.

We set off, Hanno and Abibaal sitting up behind

the old mule, Anna and I squashed among the baskets in the back. The sky was a brilliant blue and the air sweet with the taste of olives and grapes. We passed a stream of racegoers, all headed on foot towards Utica. A man walking by himself and carrying a pack waved as we trundled past.

'Any chance of a ride?'

Hanno shook his head and jerked his thumb back at the baskets and wine jars.

'Sorry. No room.'

'Understood.' The man smiled. He had an unusual voice, light and high-pitched. His dark hair was short and speckled with grey and his eyes were the same colour as the sky overhead. It felt as though he looked at me for too long, and I was glad when we were out of sight.

'I hope the hare stew won't spoil before we get back for supper,' fretted Anna. 'Dido, I'll need you to put blankets on the bed in the best bedchamber when we get back, do you think you can manage that?'

'Whose is the grave by the wood?'

Anna cast a warning glance at the boys' heads and put her finger to her lips. But the brothers were arguing over who should be holding the reins and hadn't heard me.

'That's their mother. Mistress Ayzebel,' whispered Anna.

'When did she die?'

'Just over a year ago. The baby's buried with her too. It was so sad. The master adored her, everyone did, even Nicias. The boys miss her terribly.'

I glanced at Hanno and Abibaal and felt suddenly closer to them.

We arrived in Utica to find the wide main street heaving with people. It was a large and obviously prosperous city, though the racetrack was less than half the size of the Circus Maximus, with makeshift benches on which spectators were packed in brightly coloured rows. Hanno pointed the wagon towards the warm-up area. I spotted Opellius Otho easily. He was seated in a cushioned chair that looked as if it might collapse under his weight and his sleek black head was inclined towards Scorpus, who was pointing at the pair of long-tailed greys being wheeled around the warm-up arena by Parmenion. Next to Otho and also listening to Scorpus was a short, muscular man with a weather-beaten face whom I knew to be Crito, the trainer of the Blues. I'd only ever seen him from a distance outside the Circus and thought the chances of him knowing me were luckily small, especially with my new hairstyle and clothes. Atticus said once that the only reason Crito was the most successful trainer at the Circus was because of Otho's money. But Antonius had disagreed. 'He knows a good horse when he sees one and his drivers respect him.'

Otho's eyes brightened as he saw us carrying the baskets of food towards him.

'Scorpus, my friend, what hospitality you always show me. You know the way to my heart, don't you?'

'It's your purse I'm trying to find, Otho.'

'I know it is, my old friend, I know it is, and you're doing very well.' Otho winked and pinched Anna's cheek before helping himself to one of the pastries she was offering him. His eye fell on me.

'Here's another pretty face. I don't remember her from last time.'

'Anna needed another pair of hands at home,' said Scorpus shortly. Crito was more interested in the dish of melon I was holding and barely gave me a second glance.

While Scorpus, Crito and Otho discussed horses, Anna and I served the rest of the food. Parmenion came over and helped himself to a piece of mutton pie, in defiance of Anna's protests.

'How did your race go this morning, Parmenion?' asked Hanno.

'Terribly. I was going nicely, taking the turns as clean as you like, three lengths in the lead. But a horse-fly landed on my arm, just *sat* there and didn't move. I *had* to get it off before it crawled up my sleeve; those creatures think I'm sweeter than honey. Next thing you know, I'd crashed into the fence.'

The twins collapsed into giggles. Parmenion took a bite out of the pie and grinned at me.

'Sorry about the mouse incident this morning. It wasn't my idea, I promise.'

When we had finished serving, Scorpus said that Anna and I could go to watch the races. We arrived to find Hanno and Abibaal having a fierce argument with two men who were trying to take the seats they'd been keeping for us. As the shouting escalated, Anna and I stood helplessly, wondering what to do.

Then another man sitting in the row behind spoke.

'Let the children sit down. There's plenty of room for everyone.'

I recognised the voice and turned to see the blue-eyed pedestrian who'd asked for a ride in our wagon earlier.

'No one asked you,' snarled the shorter of our two opponents.

The blue-eyed man beckoned him close and whispered in his ear. To our great surprise, the short man muttered something to his companion and they both retreated.

'How did you do that?' demanded Abibaal.

Our rescuer shrugged and smiled.

'You're very kind to help us,' said Anna. 'We saw you on the road, I'm sorry we couldn't take you in our wagon.'

'Don't mention it. I'm Cassius.' He nodded at the boys. 'Are these girls your sisters?'

He had a pleasant face, with friendly creases around his eyes. I couldn't have explained what it was about him that made me feel uneasy, just as I had on the road.

'No, this is Anna and Dido,' said Hanno by way of explanation, and the man seemed satisfied.

'It's the four-horse teams next. Anna's going to be watching this race *very* carefully,' said Abibaal.

'Oh, be quiet,' said Anna, turning red.

But I saw that her eyes lingered all the same on the charioteer who emerged from the third lane. Tall and pale-faced behind his four-horse team of dapple-greys, Antigonus was the eldest and most experienced of Scorpus's apprentices. I'd always found him silent and unfriendly in the few encounters we'd had, but he drove with a calmness and control that I knew my father would have admired. In any other company, it would be him who Hanno, Abibaal and all the other young boys in the crowd were staring at worshipfully.

But they only had eyes for one charioteer and despite my own feelings, I didn't blame them. With the possible exception of Fabius, I'd never seen anyone who handled the reins with such aggressive brilliance as Nicias. Watching his quartet of spotted ponies glide around each corner in a curl of dust, his agile brown body flexing like a bow string, I found myself thinking that this was what the boy Achilles must have driven like, in the old story Antonius used to tell me when I was little.

The field kept together for the first few laps. Then Antigonus broke from the pack just after the fifth turn, cutting inside another team with only a narrow gap to aim for.

'Oh, that looked dangerous,' squealed Anna.

'No, he had plenty of room,' I said. 'Those greys have got good foot-speed but they're not so quick on the turns. It was the right thing for Antigonus to overtake there.'

Hanno and Abibaal both looked surprised. Cassius whistled.

'Now here's a young lady who knows her horses.'

As if he'd been waiting for Antigonus to make his move, Nicias attacked too, overtaking another team so fast on the outside of the turn that the wheels of his chariot lifted off the track. The move drew admiring gasps from the spectators.

'Show-off,' said Hanno enviously.

'He's good, no doubt about it,' said Cassius. 'Needs to wind his reins tighter though. He can afford to have them loose with a well-trained team like that, but tougher horses will get away from him if he's not careful.'

I felt immediately friendlier towards him. Cassius seemed to sense my change of mood and we started to talk about what made a great charioteer. He talked so much sense that soon I was chatting away as eagerly as if he'd been my father or Atticus.

'What do you think of Fabius?' I asked.

'Talk about a great driver. He's one of the best there's ever been, no doubt about it.'

'Isn't he? Don't you love the way he makes it look so easy? Mind you, he does have the best horses with the Four Winds.'

'That's true.' Cassius paused. 'So, you're from Rome, are you?'

'What?'

'If you've seen Fabius driving the Four Winds, you must have lived in Rome. What brought you here?'

There was something about the way he said it that gave me that uneasy feeling again. A loud cheer from the crowd saved me from having to answer. Nicias was going at full pelt and the gap between him and Antigonus's greys was less than half a length, with only the last lap to go.

'Come on, Antigonus,' pleaded Anna.

My heart was with her, but I knew what the result would be. As they approached the final corner, Antigonus gave a perfect demonstration of the art of holding the inside line so that no one else could slip through. But Nicias again went to overtake on the outside. He edged past Antigonus on the straight and crossed the finishing line with his arm in the air. Antigonus's head dropped and I could feel Anna's disappointment, but the crowd yelled their appreciation for Nicias. When everyone had sat back down in their seats, I realised that Cassius was standing.

'Nice meeting you, Dido. I hope I see you again soon.'

He smiled and disappeared through the exit.

XIII

Otho raised his cup and tapped his knife against it, the noise echoing into the starlit sky and silencing the conversation.

'I hope you lads know how lucky you are, being trained by this man. I'd like you to join me in toasting my good friend Scorpus. I owe him much of my success. And one day, perhaps, so will all of you.'

'To Scorpus,' everyone chimed.

Standing just behind Otho, as instructed by Anna, I waited to clear dishes and pour more wine for anyone who wanted it. Supper had been served on the porch, with Scorpus, Otho and Crito at one end of the long table and the drivers at the other. Parmenion was throwing dates at Nicias. Antigonus wasn't talking to either of them. I guessed he was brooding about losing to Nicias. Through the doorway into the atrium I saw Hanno and Abibaal, barefoot and dressed in their sleeping tunics, sneaking back to bed after cadging scraps off Anna in the kitchen. Flies tussled with each other in the light from the oil lamps.

'I congratulate you, Scorpus,' said Otho, raising his drinking cup. 'You continue to train the finest horses in the empire.'

'Agreed,' said Crito, wiping a piece of bread in the sauce on his plate. 'Best selection we've seen on this trip.'

Scorpus nodded.

'You flatter me, both of you. I hope that means you're prepared to pay handsomely for your dinner, Otho.'

Nicias had tilted his head and I could tell that he was trying to listen to the conversation. Otho laughed.

'Let's leave the business until morning, Scorpus. I'm tired and a little drunk and you would no doubt try to fleece me on the price, even with Crito here to advise me. But your horses certainly impressed me today. As did your drivers.' Otho glanced down the table at Nicias with a knowing look that suggested he was aware the young charioteer was listening. 'Almost as much as your girl's good stew of hare.'

'I'm glad our simple food pleases you.'

'But of course. I'm a simple man, as you know, Scorpus. Give me honest fare like this over all the roasted peacock and jellied sea-urchins that my rich friends serve back in Rome.'

'Friends? I didn't know you had any, Otho.'

'Oh, not among the other faction leaders, of course.' Otho cackled. 'They all detest me, Hosidius Ruga most of all. Poor Ruga. He hopes his fortunes may change now that the Greens have such a famous supporter.'

'Who would that be, then?'

'Tiberius's heir,' said Crito. 'The one they call Caligula. Came over to the Circus from Capri about a month ago and wore a green tunic, as if he was one of the crowd.' Crito snorted. 'No prizes for guessing what he was up to. The Greens have always been the people's favourite faction.'

'Bad luck, Otho.'

Otho burped loudly.

'I'm a businessman, not a politician, Scorpus. What do I care for the people's approval, as long as I make money? But I'll tell you something. If that boy does become emperor, Rome will suffer for it.'

'You sound unusually knowledgeable.'

'Ha! People talk about Tiberius and the wicked things he's done. But believe me, they're nothing to the stories you hear about Caligula. The worst kinds of depravity you can imagine seem to be entertainment for the boy. They say he likes to watch people being tortured and executed – the more viciously, the better.'

Otho took out a silver toothpick and started to clean his teeth with it.

'What was I talking about before? Ah, my old friend, Ruga. He's really feeling the pressure from his investors. The Greens haven't had a great team or a great driver for a long time now. Then there was that unfortunate business with their trainer…'

Otho motioned to me to top up his wine. I did so with a shaking hand, sensing Scorpus's black eyes on me.

'What business was that?'

'Don't tell me you didn't hear about it? I thought you had an ear to the ground. Tell him, Crito.'

'Ruga's trainer got caught trying to fix races,' said Crito, shelling a nut with his calloused fingers as he talked. 'One of their drivers, Scylax, owned up that Antonius had offered him money to lose. Said it wasn't the first time either.'

Cold liquid spilled between my toes. The wine from the jug gushed over the trailing hem of Otho's cloak and I stammered an apology which he waved away.

'Don't worry, my dear. Those poor souls down below will be grateful for it.'

I squatted, soaking up the red wine with a napkin.

My hands wouldn't stop shaking. Otho swirled the dregs in his cup.

'Ruga claimed to be the hero of the piece, of course. Made a great show of how he got rid of this... what was his name, Crito?'

'Antonius.'

'... this Antonius as soon as he found out. Even tried to claim that I was the one who paid Antonius to do it, though he backed down when I told him to prove it.'

'The Green supporters weren't happy, as you can imagine,' said Crito. 'It's on every wall in the city now. Antonius the Traitor. Antonius the Enemy of the Greens. No one's seen him since, or his second-in-command, Atticus. Probably had to go on the run to avoid the mob tearing them apart. It's a shame. Antonius was a great driver in his day. Always thought of him as a good man.'

'Yes, I've heard other people say that,' said Otho. 'Scorpus, what about you? Did you know this Antonius?'

I looked up and saw Scorpus toying with the knife on his plate. His eyes met mine and I read disgust in them.

'No. I can't say that I did.'

XIV

I waited until Anna's breathing became slow and even. The villa was quiet apart from the distant rumble of Otho's snoring in the best bedroom. I put on my old green tunic with its faint smell of Porcellus then peeled my blanket off the mattress. It would have to do for a travelling cloak, and I would need one if I was going to be walking all night. I paused in the doorway, looking back at the still form of Anna. I wished I knew how to write so that I could say goodbye to her. Slipping into the kitchen, I picked up the cloth sack full of leftovers from Otho's dinner that I'd hidden in a cupboard.

Outside, there was a sweet smell of autumn rain in the air. Pinpricks of light from the stars glimmered in the black sky and the moon bathed the landscape with its silver beam. A rustling sound made me jump, but it was just a horse scratching its rump against a fence-post. I wanted desperately to say goodbye to Icarus. But the risk that he would wake everyone was too great. I climbed over the gate as quietly as I could and soon I was on the road to Utica.

An owl flew low overhead, disappearing into the darkness. I pulled the blanket closer about me, hitching the cloth sack over my shoulder. It was about two miles to Utica, where I knew I'd be able to find a boat going to Rome – Scorpus had talked to Otho about shipping horses from there. Maybe I'd get lucky and run into someone like Rufus again. I still had the coins he'd given me. If not, I'd have to take my chances. I raged as I remembered the contempt on Scorpus's face when Otho and Crito told him what was being said about Antonius. How dare he believe those lies about my father! Was that what Ruga had told Justus? Had Justus believed him?

I jumped at the sound of a scream from deep in the valley below. The owl must have caught its prey. A fence to my left marked the boundary of Scorpus's land. There had been children balancing on it earlier that day as we'd driven to Utica, skinny waifs belonging to the farmer who owned the pasture next door. They'd called to Hanno when they smelled the food on the wagon but he'd told them to get lost. I would have given them something from Otho's leftovers, but they'd gone by the time we got back.

Another scream rang out. Something about it made my skin prickle. I stopped and tried to see into the patchwork of fields. A noise carried on the wind, a thudding which I recognised as hooves striking turf. My first thought was that Icarus had got out of his field and was trying to follow me. I began to clamber down the side of the valley, stumbling in the gloom. Another scream, much louder than the one I'd heard from the road, made me start to run. Finally, I saw the outline of a horse on the far side of the pasture. It was thrashing about as though trying to escape its own shadow. When I got closer, I saw that it was Sciron. He must have found a way through the fence, lured by the temptation of fresh grass. His hind leg was caught in the tight loop of a snare, left in the field no doubt by those hungry children, hoping to catch a rabbit for their dinner.

'Easy, boy.' I raised my hands. 'Easy, I'll help you. Let me help you.'

I edged closer, searching for where the end of the snare was buried and trying to keep clear of Sciron's flailing hooves. He was holding one of his front legs up as though trying to launch himself forward. I trod on what felt like a length of rope and reached to pick it up. It was colder and rougher in my hand than I expected. Then I saw an eye gleaming like a jewel in the moonlight and I dropped it with a scream. The snake lay dead in the grass. Its head had been trampled into the ground. Now I understood why Sciron couldn't bear to put weight on that front leg. The snare wasn't the danger any more.

Antonius's voice suddenly filled my head. I remembered a day when I was very young and we were visiting Marius in Hispania. Teres had come running in saying that a horse had been bitten by a snake. Marius had grabbed a knife, but Antonius stopped him. *Cutting it out won't do any good,* he'd said in that strong, quiet way he had. *Once the venom's in, no sense going after it. The best thing you can do is keep the horse calm. Stop the venom spreading round the blood. The rest of it's up to the animal. If he's strong, he'll make it.*

Sciron stumbled as he landed, falling on his front knees. I hurled myself down, landing on his withers with the full weight of my body. He threw up his head, hitting me hard in the nose. I tasted blood and could barely see through tears of pain, but I fought to stop him from scrabbling to his feet again, pleading with him, desperately stroking his sweat-drenched neck.

'Please,' I whispered. 'Lie still. Lie still.'

He made a few more attempts to throw me off his back and then quite suddenly, the fight went out of him and he sank like a wounded soldier about to die on the battlefield. I could feel his flanks rising and falling. His eyes blinked despairingly in the moonlight. I crawled along to his head and put my cheek against his.

'I'll look after you,' I promised frantically.

He got upset again when I rested my hand gently on his wounded foreleg. A single touch was enough for me to feel how hot it was. The cloth sack was just within reach where I'd dropped it. I tipped out the food, twisted the sack into a bandage and tied it tightly around the top of Sciron's leg to try to stop the poison spreading. Then I took off the blanket and spread it over as much of his body as I could.

Gently, I stroked Sciron's neck. His breathing was rough and uneven. I told him that I would stay with him and that it would be all right. I kept telling him, and I didn't stop.

A hand gripped my arm. I opened my eyes, expecting to see Macro who had been chasing me through my dreams. But it was Scorpus's face above mine. Behind him, I could see Antigonus and Parmenion.

They were both staring at me. It was light and the sky was striped with the pink dawn.

Sciron's body lay motionless under my head. His heartbeat had been loud and fast the last time I heard it. Now I couldn't hear anything at all through the blanket. He was warm, though, so he couldn't have died long before Scorpus woke me.

'I'm sorry. I tried so hard,' I whispered. 'I tried to make him better, I would have come to get you, but I was worried he wouldn't make it. I'm so sorry, I tried to save him, I really did.'

I closed my eyes against the tears that came. Scorpus's hand left my arm and I felt his palm pressing gently against my cheek.

'You did save him, Dido. He's still here. He's been waiting for you to wake up.'

I opened my eyes. Sciron was twisting his head to look at me. His eyes were bright and brown. *About time*, they seemed to say.

XV

'I couldn't believe it when the master carried you in. I'd only just woken up – I didn't even realise you weren't still in bed.'

Steam clouded the kitchen as Anna poured more hot water around my feet. I was shivering so she fetched another blanket, swaddling me like a baby.

'I couldn't sleep,' I stuttered through chattering teeth.

'Praise the gods for it. You're so clever, Dido. To have known what to do. Antigonus says Sciron would have died if you hadn't been there.'

The door opened and Scorpus came in.

'How's Sciron?' I asked, noticing that he was carrying the cloth sack.

'He's lucky, that's what he is. Snake didn't get a clean bite. Wouldn't have been anything you or I could do if it had.'

He nodded to Anna.

'Take our guest his breakfast. I don't want him spending his money on an empty stomach.'

Anna squeezed my shoulder and went out.

'Is Sciron really going to be all right?' I asked again, as Scorpus tested the water before tipping in some more from the jug.

'As far as I can tell. We'll keep poulticing the leg, draw out any poison left in there. Tougher than a gladiator, old Sciron. He was the outside horse in my last winning team before I left Rome. I didn't like to leave such a good friend behind.'

I thought of Porcellus and bit my lip.

'Even so,' continued Scorpus. 'The bite would have finished him if someone hadn't been there to keep him quiet and stop the venom spreading. You saved him, Dido. That horse owes you his life. I owe you for it too.'

I watched the tears dripping off my nose into the murky water lapping at my ankles. One of Scorpus's hands, warm and rough with old blisters, covered mine. We sat there awkwardly as I tried to stifle my sobs. Then he put the sack down in front of me.

'I'm guessing you used this to carry the remains of Otho's dinner that I saw in the field. I can't pretend I'm not glad you were out there, Dido. But I wouldn't mind knowing where you were trying to get to in the middle of the night.'

'Home,' I choked.

'Back to Rome? That's a long way.'

'I have to stop them telling lies. I have to tell everyone the truth, about what happened. I know you believed what Otho and Crito said last night. But it's not true, none of it. My papa never cheated on anything. *Never.*'

'I know that, Dido. I'm sorry you thought I didn't.'

'But...' I blinked at him through my tears. 'I thought you weren't friends. Papa said so.'

'That's true enough. We weren't friends. But I'd never believe any man who told me Antonius was a cheat. He fought fairly. Even if we were on opposite sides.'

'So why didn't you tell them that?' I demanded. 'Why didn't you say that you thought Ruga was lying?'

'I knew Nicias was listening to a lot of what we were saying last night. I didn't want him or anyone else to make the connection between you and Antonius. All they know is that you're the daughter of someone I used to race against, and that's all they need to know.'

I watched the steam rising from my feet.

'I didn't tell you about Papa because I didn't know if I could trust you.'

'Will you trust me now? You can, you know.'

It all came pouring out then. My last night in Rome, the jar I'd found in Nessus's stable, Antonius's confrontation with Ruga and Macro killing my father. Scorpus stood up and ran his hand over his stubbled chin.

'This berry you found. Was it red, like you find on a yew tree?'

'Yes. Do you know what it was?'

'I could be wrong, but it sounds like ephedron.'

'What's that?'

'Not something you find growing on trees around the Field of Mars. More like from an apothecary in Thieves Street. Your father would have known exactly what it was as soon as he saw it. The brew from the stems does something strange to horses, opens up the lungs, makes them run faster. Can kill them if you give them too much.'

'That's horrible. Poor Nessus. No wonder he was acting so strangely. I *told* Justus there was something wrong with him.'

'Who's Justus?'

'A friend,' I muttered. 'So, do you think it was Macro who gave the ephedron to Ruga?'

'Sounds like it, though Macro probably got the drug from someone else, someone who knew what they were doing. Takes a lot of skill to brew it right.'

'How do *you* know so much about it?'

'Drugging horses, to win or to lose, used to be a big problem at the Circus. The factions came down hard on it. But if Ruga's got money problems, like Otho said, then it would have been an easy way to fix them. Maybe he and this Macro had a deal to share the profits.'

'I'm worried that they might still be trying to find me.'

Scorpus shook his head.

'You've been here for over a month. Do you really think that the head of the emperor's own bodyguard wouldn't have been able to find you if he wanted to?'

I considered this.

'Believe me, Dido. Why would they think a young girl like you could hurt them? You're safe here. I don't want you to think about running away again. I'm sorry that I haven't made you feel as welcome as I should have. I...'

He broke off and stared at the kitchen floor. Then, abruptly, he left the room. When he came back, he put something into my hand. It was a little wooden horse, whittled from a piece of cedar.

'This isn't much of a thank you for what you did. But I'd like you to have it. From Sciron and me. I carved it myself when I was about your age, from an old branch that fell in the woods.'

'Who is it?'

'His name was Tigris. An old pony my father used to own. My brothers and sisters and I would take turns to race him when we were young, imagining we were at the Circus Maximus.'

I propped up the pony in my palm, tracing my finger over its finely carved mane.

'From tomorrow, I'd like you to help with the horses,' said Scorpus. 'Grooming, feeding, doing whatever you used to do for your father. Would that make you happier?'

I wondered for a moment if I should tell him about my secret training sessions with Icarus but decided against it.

'The boys won't like it.'

'Don't be so sure about that. Parmenion and Antigonus are very impressed by how you saved Sciron.'

Nicias won't be, I thought. I looked up at Scorpus and to my surprise saw a glint of humour in his eyes.

'It's for Anna's sake as much as anyone's. She says she's never met anyone who peels onions the way you do.'

I felt an answering smile tugging at my lips.

XVI

'**A**gain.'

Nicias tugged viciously on the inside rein attached to Icarus's bridle.

'This animal is lazy and stupid,' he screamed.

'You're rushing him,' replied Scorpus. 'Take him round again and this time, forget about speed. It's all about your positioning.'

I watched anxiously as Nicias steered the training chariot in a tight circle. It was a tricky task that Scorpus had set. The aim was to drive a single chariot cleanly between ten pairs of flimsy wooden pyramids which had been laid out in a narrow twisting pattern. Not only did you have to complete the course without knocking over a pyramid, you had to do it before all the water ran out of the hole in the earthenware pot which Hanno was holding. Neither Antigonus with Snowy, nor Parmenion with Perdix had managed it. Now they were sitting on the fence observing Nicias's attempt. I was sure that Icarus could do it. I was still training him in secret every morning. But he was terrified of Nicias and never went well for him.

Once again, Nicias pointed Icarus at the first set of pyramids. Once again, Icarus swerved out of the turn, shaking his head and rolling his eyes. Parmenion cheered loudly. Nicias cursed.

'All right. Enough for tonight,' said Scorpus, sounding weary. 'You three, help get them in.'

He nodded at Abibaal, Hanno and me. The boys raced each other for the right to stable Perdix, who was their favourite. I ducked under the fence, anxious to get Icarus away from Nicias.

'Useless,' he was saying to Scorpus as I approached. 'Completely useless. You must have been crazy to buy him.'

He stepped off the chariot and threw the end of the reins at me. I started unbuckling Icarus's bridle at once, loosening the pressure on his reddened mouth. He was sweating, his eyes wide and frightened.

'He's not a bad horse, he just needs more time,' said Scorpus.

'I'm tired of driving these donkeys. I want my chance against the best charioteers and the best teams at the Circus Maximus.'

'Your time will come.' Scorpus turned away but Nicias wasn't finished.

'Why didn't you sell me to Otho? I know he made you an offer. I could have been driving for the Blues now. You're holding me back.'

'I've told you.' There was an edge to Scorpus's voice now. 'You'll get your chance. But as I said to Otho, you've still got a lot to learn.'

Nicias stared savagely after Scorpus as he walked away. He noticed me watching.

'What are you looking at? Little man-girl, trying to do a boy's work. Scorpus should send you back to the kitchen where you belong. Get that donkey of yours out of my sight before I take this whip to him.'

Back at the stable, Icarus shied at every distraction and wouldn't let me put honey on his lip. I finished my chores before looking in on Sciron's stall. Scorpus was there, soaking linen cloths in a pail of what looked like wine and wrapping them around Sciron's front hoof. Sciron started to walk forward when he saw me until Scorpus barked at him to stay still. I rested my elbows on the door to the stall.

'How's the leg?'

'Fine. Just inflamed. Probably a bit of poison lurking in the wound. Best cure for snake-bite is black cumin through the nostrils, but he'd bite my hand off if I tried that. This is vinegar with rue flowers and thyme. Should work almost as well.'

'Can I help?'

'If you want to.'

Sciron pushed his nose into my armpit and started chewing on the sleeve of my tunic as I kneeled in the straw. I began passing cloths to Scorpus, swirling them in the pungent liquid to make sure they were properly drenched.

'Icarus would go much better if you took that curb-bit out of his mouth,' I said.

'It'll stop hurting once the horse does as he's told.'

'He's terrified of Nicias. Why don't you let Antigonus drive him?'

'If he ever gets to the Circus, he's going to have to be willing to go for whoever's driving him. Better he learns that here and now, under my eye. Besides, he's already improved a lot this past month.'

Because of me, not you, I wanted to tell him.

'I bet Sciron didn't go well for everyone who drove him.'

'True,' said Scorpus. 'But Sciron could take care of himself. If he didn't like his driver, he'd let them know about it.'

'He must have liked you.'

'We understood each other.'

'How old were you when you got your first race at the Circus?'

'Sixteen, maybe seventeen.'

'What was the result?'

'I won.'

I paused in the middle of squeezing out a cloth.

'You won your first ever race at the Circus Maximus? Are you serious?'

Scorpus shrugged. 'I had a good team.'

His words awoke a memory.

'Papa used to say the difference between a good charioteer and a great one is that a great charioteer can win even when he doesn't have the best horses.'

'I wouldn't disagree with that.'

'He said the only way he could ever beat *you* was if he had better horses.'

'That was nice of him,' said Scorpus after a pause. 'But he beat me often enough. And not always with great horses.'

He held out his hand for another cloth which I passed to him promptly, hoping that if I were particularly helpful, I might have a better chance of getting the answer I was hoping for from my next question.

'Would you teach me to drive a four?'

'No.'

It was the answer I'd expected but I still felt irritated.

'Why not?'

'When was the last time you saw a girl driving in the Circus?'

'I'm not asking to drive in the Circus,' I said as reasonably as I could. 'I just want to learn to handle a four. I already know how to drive a pair, Papa taught me.'

'Then it sounds like you already know more than you need.'

He finished swaddling Sciron's hoof then tipped the rest of the vinegar out of the bucket into the straw.

'These aren't toy animals we're training, Dido. They're the best racehorses money can buy and they're going to race for the best teams, for the best drivers. I'm not going to risk their sale price by letting a girl spoil them.'

He looked at me in that way he had where I could never tell if he was being cold or sympathetic.

'It's a dangerous game, Dido, and with all due respect to your father, it's a man's game. A girl just wouldn't be strong enough to handle a team. You're good with them in the stable, more than good, I'll give you that. Stick to grooming them, taking care of them and healing their wounds when they're sick. You're more use to them that way.'

'If you didn't use such a horrible bit on them, there wouldn't be so many wounds for me to heal.'

'Don't start this again, Dido.'

'My father would have said yes.'

It was childish of me to say it, I knew. I could tell at once by the hardening of his jaw that I had pushed him too far.

'I'm not your father, am I?'

He unlatched the door of the stall and closed it behind him.

against Incitatus though. Still, you've got to die somehow, haven't you?'

I must have looked bewildered because Helix laughed.

'You new bloods. A few wins at your local track and you think the Circus will be just the same. Incitatus is the emperor's horse. The Greens' champion.'

I was curious.

'Does Fabius drive him?' I asked.

Helix laughed again.

'Fabius? Where did you hear about that old has-been? The Greens' number one is Nicias. He drives Incitatus.'

I felt the hairs on my arms prickle. Helix leaned in.

'Take my advice. You ever find yourself in a race with Nicias, stay out of his way. He likes to shipwreck people. Particularly new bloods.'

He straightened up and winked at me. 'Now make sure you pay attention in training today.'

He strolled away, leaving me with a feeling of dread.

'Are you sure it's him?' whispered Parmenion.

'Has to be,' I whispered, 'Helix says he's their best driver and he likes to shipwreck people.'

Antigonus grunted. 'Sounds like Nicias.'

We were sitting in the spectators' stand at the Trigarium, the practice track on the Field of Mars shared by all the factions between race days. The late afternoon sun was on our backs as we watched Crito putting each of the new recruits through their paces. I'd already done laps with three different sets of horses and thought I'd managed them pretty well, but the idea of Nicias being in Rome was all I could think about.

'What if he recognises me?'

'Not a chance,' said Parmenion. 'Have you seen yourself lately?'

Crito came over to us.

'Good work today, boys. Antigonus, you're going in race four tomorrow. Parmenion, Leon, I've got you both in race six. The horses you brought with you need more time to settle in, so you'll all be driving new teams. But I like what I saw today. Scorpus has done a fine job with you lads.'

After training was over, I managed to slip away from Antigonus and Parmenion and headed towards the open parkland adjoining the Trigarium where hundreds of Circus horses grazed in fenced-off pastures. Armed guards employed by the factions watched over them and I did my best not to attract attention while I strained my eyes in search of a familiar black head with a white star. But there was no sign of Porcellus. With a heavy heart, I followed the bend of the river until I reached the spot where Antonius and I used to try in vain to catch wolf-fish. Edging down the bank, I sat and stared into the yellow water.

'I made it, Papa. I'm here,' I said. 'Tomorrow I'm going to race at the Circus Maximus. I told you I'd do it one day.'

I tried to laugh but my throat was too tight.

'Do you remember telling me about your great rival, Scorpus of the Blues? He's the one who's kept me safe all this time. I'm afraid I persuaded him to teach me how to drive a four. Sometimes I feel as if you're with me, so maybe you already know that. I'm sorry you and Scorpus weren't friends. I think you would be if you met now.'

A couple wandered past, obviously looking for a quiet place to be romantic. I waited for them to walk by, then reached behind my neck and undid the clasp of the silver chain. Holding the crescent that had once belonged to my mother in the flat of my hand, I brushed my thumb over the little 'S' and kissed it.

'Scorpus told me you used to wear this during races and that it made you feel like Mama was with you. So I want you to have it now. Tigris will take care of me.'

Quickly, so that I wouldn't lose my resolve, I let the necklace slip through my fingers and watched it sink beneath the water, fighting the impulse to dive in after it.

'I love you, Papa,' I whispered. 'I promise I'm going to win for you.'

Hours seemed to pass before I was able to drag myself to my feet. I wiped my face on my sleeve and made my way back to the Blues' club-house. It was late evening now and the city was alive with the party atmosphere that always gripped Rome on the eve of race days. Stable Street was crowded with revellers, tourists and street traders, mingling beneath the coloured flags of the factions. Two gangs of Green and Blue supporters were confronting each other outside a tavern, exchanging insults and spoiling for a fight. I spotted Antigonus and Parmenion having a drink with some other charioteers and hurried past, not wanting them to see me.

As I neared the Blues' side gate, I stepped back to let a horse and cart pass. There was always a lot of traffic on this street at night. Some were rubbish carts, others were supply vehicles like this one, bringing stores of hay and grain to the club-houses. The cart pulled up short of the big gate leading into the Blues' stable yard. It was drawn by a skinny horse with a straggly mane and leather blinkers over its eyes. In the dark, I couldn't make out its colour though I could see its ribs through its dirty coat. But something about the shape of the head seemed familiar. Grooms in blue uniform emerged from the yard and began unloading sacks from the rear of the cart. The horse was stubbornly resisting the driver's attempts to move him further down the street. A groom came to help but no sooner had he taken the bridle than he snatched his hand back with an oath. The driver lashed the animal with his whip. It reared and plunged forward, sending pedestrians diving out of the way. The grooms and the driver pursued the runaway vehicle along the narrow street, and I could hear their shouts and curses well after they'd vanished from sight. I went up to my little cell and for a long time was unable to sleep, wondering where I'd seen that horse before.

XXVIII

'Race five! Race five! Chariots ready!'

Three more charioteers got up to leave, receiving slaps on the back from Helix and some of the veterans gathered by the door. I took a deep breath, waiting for the waves in my stomach to settle. The changing room was crowded, and I shrank against the wall as a sweat-soaked body squeezed past me. A few who had already raced were relaxing in the cold plunge pool in the middle of the room. Their nakedness didn't embarrass me. I was used to it after three years among the boys at Utica. I only wished I could get into the water and cool myself down as well. My blue tunic was sticking to my back and the bandages flattening my chest were drenched.

Next to me, Parmenion was attempting to put his tunic on but kept getting it stuck on his head. He'd been cracking jokes all morning as usual, but

I could see that his hands were shaking. We both looked up as Antigonus came in, his face covered in sweat and sand, his blue race tunic torn at the neck.

'How did you do?' asked Parmenion.

Antigonus collapsed on the bench next to us and shook his head. He looked exhausted.

'It's brutal out there, absolutely brutal. I finished, which is something. My inside horse almost lost a leg. They're not being very thorough about clearing the debris from the track.'

'Who won?'

'One of the Green teams. That's four wins out of four for them so far today. The Reds and Whites are making a competition of it behind them, but the Blues are nowhere.'

A stretcher was carried in bearing an unconscious charioteer, his face covered in blood. The faction doctor followed close behind and some of the other drivers crowded round.

'What happened?'

'Greens shipwrecked him.'

'Who was it? That scumbag Nicias?'

'No, he's not out until later. The Greens always put him and Incitatus last so the crowd stays to watch.'

A stable boy poked his head through the doorway of the changing room.

'Race six! Chariots ready.'

My stomach turned over. Parmenion groaned.

'Good luck,' said Antigonus, handing me my helmet. 'Remember what Scorpus said and don't go for glory in your first race. Just get back alive.'

As Parmenion and I passed Helix and the older charioteers standing at the door, I felt their amused eyes on us.

'Remember what I said, now,' murmured Helix.

We emerged into the light and the small crowd of Blues' supporters gathered outside the changing room stared at us without enthusiasm. A girl in a low-cut dress said something to Parmenion, who looked more cheerful. I glanced over at the Greens' stables opposite. A huge crowd was surrounding them. I could just see the heads of some of their charioteers as they stepped up on to their chariots.

Parmenion swore as he walked straight into the back of me. The girl he was flirting with laughed.

'Watch where you're going, Di— I mean, Leon.'

I barely heard him. I'd been looking for Porcellus. Instead, my eye was drawn to a burly man in a white tunic, standing to the side of the crowd, talking to a smaller man with a bald head. Instantly, the noise of the forum seemed to fade. My chest tightened, as if someone was holding me under water.

'What's going on with you?' asked Parmenion.

'Nothing,' I muttered. 'Just thought I was going to be sick.'

'You and me both. Come on. Let's get this over with.'

I kept close to Parmenion. My view of Macro and Charicles was now blocked by the crowd of Blues' grooms preparing the horses. One nodded to me.

'Are you Leon? That's your team there.'

I stared at the quartet of horses lined up in front of me. Was he joking?

'Who put them together?'

The groom shrugged.

'Otho's had to sell so many horses. We have to make teams out of what we've got.'

They were the worst-matched four I'd ever seen. The two yoke horses were a dusty brown and at least a hand shorter than the inside horse, a skewbald whose plaits were already coming undone. The outside horse was a tall, fine-boned grey with sleepy eyes.

'What are their names?' I asked the groom, who obviously thought I was mad for wanting to know.

'Patch, Swift, Lightning and Silver. Use plenty of whip on Silver. He's lazy.'

An engineer arrived and made a few checks of my chariot. While he did his work, I quickly undid some of Patch's plaits and retied them. There was no way I was going out in the Circus Maximus for the first time with a horse as badly turned out as that. The four of them were led into harness, the big grey Silver dragging his hooves when it came to his turn. I took a deep breath and stepped on to the springs of the chariot. From here, I could see over the heads of the vast crowd in the forum. Macro and Charicles had both disappeared. I told myself to relax. The groom did a final check.

'There you go. Warm-up's that way.'

We moved off in procession through the gap that had been cleared for us. Parmenion was ahead of me, driving three chestnuts matched with a red roan. When we reached the warm-up enclosure alongside the start gates, the three Red and three White teams were already thundering around the outside of the track, driven by hard-looking men whose bulging arm and leg muscles were hatched with old scars. Their pace was terrifying. Trying not to seem intimidated, I followed Parmenion into the enclosure.

After one lap, I knew I stood no chance. Patch was a nervous horse who shied at everything while whoever had named Swift and Lightning had obviously been making a bad joke. As for Silver, he had a good, fast stride but it was completely the wrong length for his shorter teammates and we kept on losing rhythm.

'Get out of it, new blood!' someone bellowed as they barged past, almost clipping my wheels. I was startled to glimpse the ugly, brutish face of Scylax and felt a sudden surge of hatred, remembering the lie he had told about Antonius. Scylax caught up to his brother, Darius, who had just entered the arena. The pair of them spoke to each other and glanced back at me. Helix's warning echoed through my head.

'Race six! In for the draw!'

We all pulled our sweating horses in front of the lane steward. The urn was tipped and a blue ball drawn. The steward glanced at the number on it, nodded at me and held up a finger to the crowd.

'One.'

My stomach lurched. Lane one was the most dangerous draw, with the greatest risk of being pushed into the channel as the horses fought for position on the opening lap.

A groom came to lead my team through the first of the twelve arches to the starting gates. The outer door shut behind us with a clang. I grabbed at the reins, wrapping them around my waist as fast as I could and checking that my knife was correctly stowed. It was stiflingly hot under the archway and the stench of dung made it hard to breathe. The noise of the crowd echoed through the cells. One by one, the other teams were loaded through the gates. Parmenion was at the other end of the row. Lane two to my right remained empty, for which I was grateful. It meant I would have a bit more space as we reached the break point. Groping for the wooden form of Tigris tied to Anna's ribbon, I squeezed him tightly and kissed him for luck.

I waited for the sound of the countdown overhead. Behind me, someone was shouting and arguing with the stewards. Then with a clattering of hooves, four beautiful dapple-greys barged into the starting gate to my right. I glanced across and nearly dropped the reins. In the third lane, Scylax laughed.

'Overslept again, Fabius? Probably not used to finding yourself out this early.'

'Get stuffed.'

I felt my jaw drop. What had happened to the handsome idol of my childhood? Fabius's heroic profile was now spoiled by the fold of a double chin. His hair was still black and his figure tall and upright, but even a loose-fitting green tunic couldn't disguise his rounded belly. He sensed me looking at him and scowled.

'What are you looking at, little fish?'

I felt myself turning red and looked away quickly. Overhead, the muffled sound of footsteps on the platform signalled that the start officials were in place. The chatter of the crowd was overtaken by a low chorus of anticipation that seemed to echo from the ground beneath the horses' feet. Seeing Fabius doing the same thing, I put one foot in front of the other and held the reins taut, bracing myself for the vital moment. Above, the starter counted down with stamps of his foot.

Five. Four. Three. Two.

One.

Light flooded the cell as the gates snapped back. A roar filled my ears and I was dragged into a storm.

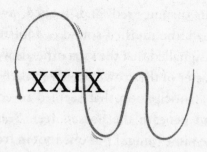

XXIX

I bathed in the hot glare of thousands of eyes upon me, saw the long ravine of track stretching out with the perfect oval of blue sky above and the bronze turning pillars in the distance.

Then the image dissolved in a cloud of sand and fury. Out of the corner of my eye, I could see a line of horses surging forward like the crest of a wave about to crash on to the shore. Patch snatched for his head. The reins slid through my damp palms, but I just managed to control my team so that we cut safely inside the channel. Fabius's greys had already pulled ahead by half a length. He might have lost his good looks, but he still drove beautifully, standing tall and balanced on the axle of the chariot.

Ahead, the white chalk line across the track that marked the point where we could break from our lanes was fast approaching. I could hear Scorpus's voice in my head. *This is where things are going to get ugly. Whatever you do, don't get boxed in or you'll hit the channel.* I waited for my wheels to cross the chalk, then pulled hard on the rein to move into the gap left by Fabius's chariot. Too hard. The chariot tilted, the wheel lifting off the track. I lost my balance and for a terrifying moment we rolled along on one wheel, only the reins wrapped around my waist saving me from falling into the tangle of galloping hooves.

The crowd was screaming. I knew they were Green supporters, hungry for a crash. But some god answered my prayer and as the horses veered left again, the chariot righted itself with a thud. My team were weaving across the track in confusion. My mistake had cost us three lengths on the rest of the field, who were rounding the first turn at the far end of the channel like a swerving flock of birds. A wheel flew across the track and a Blue charioteer hit the ground. *Parmenion*, I thought in horror. Then I saw it was our teammate, crawling on his hands and knees, the ends of his severed reins trailing across the sand. Blood poured from a deep gash in his head, trickling between his eyes. I had to change course to avoid him.

On the next straight, I caught up with Parmenion. 'You all right?' he yelled.

I nodded and we kept side by side at the back. It gave us a good view of what was going on. By the time the first dolphin's tail had flipped up, the Greens' tactics had become clear. Fabius's job was to lead the race and he was already well out in front. Darius and Scylax meanwhile were eliminating as many other charioteers as they could. Each time they clashed with a Red or White chariot, sending its driver sprawling or smashing the vehicle to pieces, there was a scream of delight from the Green supporters that easily overcame the protests of everyone else in the crowd. I said a silent prayer of thanks for Scorpus's pyramid training as we dodged the debris and wounded charioteers that kept appearing on the track.

'What are your horses like?' yelled Parmenion.

'Drunken donkeys,' I shouted back.

'Mine aren't drunk. They're sick.'

We completed the second and then the third laps. I was starting to get a feel for my mismatched team. By keeping Silver on a short outside rein and leaving my other rein loose, I had them in a better rhythm. Avoiding the missiles thrown by the crowd was another difficulty. Several rocks flew past my head and I heard Parmenion swear as one of them hit him on the hand. He waved his injured fist at the crowd.

'Come on then, we'll take on the lot of you!'

Four dolphins down and half the field had either crashed or been forced to retire. Parmenion and I, together with a White charioteer were now the only challengers left in the race with the Greens. I saw Darius glance behind him. He signalled to Scylax, who started to drop back.

'I'll distract him,' shouted Parmenion.

I shook my head in protest, but he had already peeled away towards the other side of the track. As the Green chariot drew level, Parmenion took out his knife and waved it theatrically at Scylax. There was a laugh and a cheer from some in the crowd. Scylax responded by driving into the nearside of Parmenion's chariot. Their wheels clashed and a shower of sparks flew. Parmenion gestured wildly at me.

I urged my four forward. They responded well but as we made the turn into the fifth lap, the galloping hooves of Scylax's pair came up fast behind. I searched for Parmenion and saw him limping off the track on the far side of the Circus. Scylax's chariot drew level with mine and I looked into his ugly, doglike face, almost daring him to recognise me.

'Welcome to the Circus Maximus.'

The tail of his whip darted at me like a snake's tongue. I ducked in time so that it missed my eye, but my neck felt the sting of the lash. The blows kept raining down, on my head, on my arms and my back, bringing tears to my eyes. I tried to move out, but I was boxed in against the channel. The crowd were screaming their approval, like witnesses at an execution. Just as I felt I couldn't take the pain any more, Scylax switched his attention to my horses. Silver lashed his tail and squealed in outrage as the tip of the whip caught him on the nose.

'Stop it!' I screamed, forgetting to disguise my voice. 'Stop it!'

Then I spotted the broken wheel ahead. Scylax was so busy trying to flay my horses that he hadn't noticed it. I hugged the inside of the track, leaving Scylax to his fate. Too late, he saw it coming. His chariot burst apart, showering me in wooden splinters. There was a roar around the stadium. I couldn't tell if it was a cheer from the Blues or a cry of protest from the Greens. Twisting round, I saw Scylax on the ground, his horses cantering free from the shattered chariot.

Darius and the White charioteer were in my sights. *Go on, Dido*, I heard Antonius whisper in my ear. Blinking away the tears, I crouched low and shook the reins. Silver's head came up and to my surprise, he responded to the signal. Brown, white and grey manes dancing, we flew down the long eastern straight of the Circus, the rushing air bringing cool relief to the burning pain on my arms and neck. My heart lifted as the Blue supporters in the crowd started to make themselves heard. We overtook the White charioteer, who was labouring now and had fallen behind Darius. Six dolphins down. One more to go.

At the other end of the stadium, Fabius was already making his penultimate turn before the finish. Darius looked behind and noticed for the first time that it wasn't his brother who was getting a cheer from the crowd. He reined in his team, waiting for me to make up the ground, then started to angle his chariot straight at me. I tried to send him the wrong way, veering first towards the outside of the track and then cutting back. But Darius lashed his four into a frenzy and drew alongside me once more, steering aggressively into my racing line.

I glanced down. My left wheel was rattling along no more than a foot's width from the channel. If it struck the stone wall, at this speed, my whole chariot would shatter into a thousand fragments just as Scylax's had done. Darius's inside horse was almost touching flanks with Silver and the pair of them flattened their ears, snarling and lunging at each other. As the bay turned its head, I saw that its eyes were bulging crazily.

The final turn was almost upon us. I prayed for it to come quickly, tightening my grip on the reins, fixing my eyes on the critical point when I knew I had to give Patch the command. Darius was so close to me that I could smell the sweat coming off him as he lashed his bays with the full force of his arm.

Then, as if a god had reached down and plucked them from the track, they weren't there any more. The way ahead was clear and as Patch nosed around the last turn, I looked across the channel and caught a brief glimpse of horses and chariot sprawled on the ground in a tangle of limbs and leather. They disappeared from view. I galloped the last long straight unopposed, made the final turn and crossed the finish line.

There was a strange silence from the crowd. I peered up into the sea of faces and saw a few blue flags being waved near the top of the Circus. Otherwise, people were quiet, not grumbling, not jeering, just quiet. Some of the Green spectators were craning their heads back towards the far end of the track, where Darius had fallen. I heard the rattle of wheels behind me. It was Fabius, already at the end of his lap of honour. Controlling his horses with one hand, he looked down at me and to my amazement, he winked. I recognised the hero of my childhood again.

'Not bad. For a little fish.'

Reaching out, he took my wrist and raised my arm in salute to the crowd. There was a pause. Then someone started clapping. Row by row, the applause spread throughout the whole Circus and I could see the Blues' supporters getting to their feet, urged on by Otho, resplendent as a peacock in the front row of his hospitality box. In a daze, I obeyed Fabius's gesture to follow him on another lap of honour, and the cheering grew even louder. Patch, Swift, Lightning and Silver looked about in wide-eyed bewilderment, clearly unused to such a reception. As we reached the far end of the track, I saw the wreckage from Darius's crash. His chariot was on its side and Darius was being treated by medics while his horses were cut from the traces. One of the bays had got up and was trying to disentangle itself, clearly badly shaken. Another lay lifeless on the track. A vet squatted over him.

'What happened?' I asked, pulling up as Fabius drove on.

The vet shook his head.

'Heart's given out. Third of the Greens' horses I've seen like it this month. Suppose it doesn't matter when you can replace them so easily.'

Some track hands were tying ropes to the animal's legs. Just before someone threw a piece of cloth over its body, I saw the thick layer of foam all over its coat, the look of excited terror frozen in its eyes.

XXX

'You see? The Blues are coming about!'

Otho was standing in his hospitality box above the pit, encouraging the cheers of the Blues' supporters. My teammates in the pit, Parmenion included, were punching me so hard on the shoulders that my arms were starting to feel numb. Crito clapped me on the back, a wide smile on his face.

'Well done, young Leon. Great racing. No one except Helix has done better than third in the last few games. You did Scorpus proud.'

Next to Otho, Helvia was fanning herself in the shade of a canopy being held by a pair of slaves. She smiled down at me like a sleepy cat. A group of children were leaning over the barrier that separated the crowd from the track, trying to get my attention. I went over to the edge of the pit, letting them grab at my tunic and touch my hands.

'What's your name? Where are you from? Are they going to put you up against Incitatus now?' The questions poured out with no pause for any answers. Then they all started jumping up and down again.

'Helix, Helix!'

I felt a hand grip my shoulder. Helix bared his gold teeth at me.

'Just been down at the stables, talking to my old teammate, Fabius,' he said. 'You've made a friend there. He said the only thing that would have made him enjoy that race more is if he'd had a better view of Scylax hitting the dirt.'

The crowd started to cheer as the horses for the final race of the day emerged from the east gate for a parade lap.

'Poor old Fabius,' continued Helix. 'Hard not to feel a little sorry for him. He thought he was going be the Greens' number one when he moved there. Hasn't worked out that way.' He nodded at the track. 'Here comes the reason why.'

I almost didn't hear him over the ecstatic roar that went up from the wall of Green spectators on the opposite side of the Circus. A team of four black horses had burst into the arena like a stormy wave across a calm surf. Their driver wore a bright green tunic and a gold helmet. A shiver passed from my head to my toes. Nicias drove just the same as he always did, standing right to the front of his chariot, his back slightly hunched, elbows sticking out aggressively either side. His whip whirled several times as he lashed his four to a gallop. Aside from maybe the Four Winds, I'd never seen horses move so fast. They rounded the turning post, and suddenly, with a shock that felt like being drenched in ice water, I saw it. The inside horse had a white star in the middle of his forehead.

'Incitatus! Incitatus!' the Green supporters screamed.

My insides convulsed. He was bigger, of course, more muscled than he used to be, with a sleek, glossy coat instead of his old peat-soft pelt. But it was Porcellus. My beautiful Porcellus, no mistaking him. The trio alongside him were magnificent animals, but there was no doubt who the star of the team was. He looked as though he could burst out of the harness and go twice as fast if the shackles were taken off him. Nicias raised his whip arm in arrogant salute. Following the direction of his gaze, high towards the top of the Circus in the middle of a sea of green, I saw a tall, slender figure standing in the imperial box, applauding wildly with both hands above his head.

Pushing through the crush of trainers, engineers and faction hands crowding the pit, I reached the side of the track just as Nicias was approaching. Porcellus's name formed on my lips, and I put up my arm and waved it, as though somehow there was a chance that he would see me, ignore Nicias's commands and come rushing over, demanding his fig like he always used to. But he didn't so much as turn his head. Four horses dashed past, their black noses darting in rhythm like four striking cobras, and I was left staring into a cloud of dust.

XXXI

All the lamps on the top floor of the Greens' club-house had been lit and the sound of music mingled with the babble of voices inside. The usual crowd of faction followers huddled in the street, hoping for a glimpse of their idols through the upstairs windows. I kept my head down as I passed the guards on duty by the club-house gate and avoided the clutches of a drunk who tried to grab my ankles as I walked past. When I was clear of the crowd, I glanced back. The guards were standing over the drunk, shouting at him to move along. I stepped into a side alley and pulled off my cloak. My green stable uniform had been too big for me when I had last worn it. Now it fitted perfectly.

After a long wait, the vehicle I was hoping for arrived. It stopped by the delivery entrance to the stables and several grooms in green uniform started to unload the sacks. I waited for the right moment then slipped out of the alley. Hoisting a sack over my shoulder, I followed the grooms into the Greens' stable yard. The fig I had taken from the Blues' mess table knocked against my hip, keeping time with the pounding of my heart. I stole a quick look around. It was the strangest feeling being here again, in the place that had been my whole world as a child.

The grooms were dumping their sacks in the corner of the feed store before heading to the street for more. It was a cavernous room at the corner of the first stable block, with barrels of grain stacked against the walls. A slave was standing with his back to me, grinding something with a pestle and mortar. There was an enormous pot bubbling over a brazier at his side. I dropped my sack on top of the pile then pretended to be retying the lace on my sandal so that I could watch what the slave was doing. He stopped pounding and picked up a wooden stick to stir the simmering contents of the pot. A tangle of what looked like frail reeds clung to the stick and a warm, bitter smell filled the air. The slave tipped more of the crushed reeds from the mortar into the pot. I looked at the sacks that had been carried in. Through a torn corner, I could see the stalks of a greyish-green plant sticking out, dry and fine like a horse's tail, a few with small red berries attached. I plucked some off just as I heard voices close by.

'It's no good having what you need if you can't do your job right. You're costing us a fortune in dead horses, Charicles.'

'The emperor expects too much. He wants the Greens to win every time, I am having to give these horses more ephedron than is good for them. It is too much pressure for me, you must talk to him.'

Charicles and Macro had stopped outside the door. Heart pounding, I walked away rapidly, passing the stable hands who were returning with more sacks. I pretended to be heading to the street but instead darted through the entrance into the stable blocks, picking up an empty bucket so that I could make an excuse about where I was going if asked. Horses whickered from either side. Several times I almost lost courage. But I was too close to seeing him again.

There was no sign of Porcellus in the first block or the second. I entered the third and when I reached the middle of the walkway, I stopped. I had come to an enormous stall, at least three times the size of the others. The doors were made from what appeared to be marble, framed with columns as though it were a little temple. Laurel wreaths hung on either side. I checked around me before taking the fig from my pocket. The stall was in darkness.

'Porcellus,' I whispered.

I couldn't see to the back. But there was a horse in there, I was sure of it. I put my hand on the latch.

'Hey. What do you think you're doing?'

Two figures in white uniform had appeared at the entrance to the block. My knuckles were bloodless as they gripped the latch.

'I'm sorry… I wanted to give this to the emperor's horse.'

One of the Praetorians beckoned to me and took the fig, examining the wrinkled purple skin. He had small eyes, narrowed in suspicion.

'No one feeds Incitatus except Charicles or the emperor. It's the rule.'

'I'm new here.'

I sneaked another glance to see if Porcellus's head had appeared. He always used to be restless when he was stabled, wanting to look out and see what was going on in the yard. Why wouldn't he come to the door when he heard my voice?

'I'm sorry,' I repeated. 'I didn't know. I'll go.'

I started to walk away.

'Wait. Stay where you are.'

My shoulders tensed. The Praetorian was speaking to his companion.

'I don't like his story. Go get the master.'

The second Praetorian disappeared. Trying not to panic but desperately searching for an escape route if the opportunity arose, I noticed that the little window of the apartment that Antonius and I had once shared was in darkness. The Praetorian returned, accompanied by a smartly dressed young man with dark wavy hair.

'What is it, Pollio?'

'This boy was trying to feed Incitatus. He says he works here, but I've never seen him before.'

The dark-haired young man was frowning at me, no trace of recognition in his eyes. Seeing him about to open his mouth, I spoke quickly.

'You do know me, Master Justus. Remember?'

XXXII

Justus still looked puzzled and for a moment, I
thought that he was going to let me down.

'I don't think I...'

I smiled at him. His jaw dropped open slightly.
He didn't look so different, I thought. Taller,
squarer in the jaw, and wider in the chest. There
were shadows under his eyes which made him
look tired. But otherwise, he was as handsome as I
remembered. I would have laughed out loud at the
expression on his face if the Praetorians hadn't been
standing there.

'Yes, of course. Of course.' To my relief, Justus
seemed to regain his senses. 'No need to worry,
Pollio. We took on some new stable hands and...
haven't had time to tell them the rules yet. You can
go back to your post now.'

Pollio didn't look entirely satisfied. Justus
clicked his fingers in my direction.

'You. Make yourself useful and come and deliver a letter for me.'

I followed him towards the club-house. He didn't look back as he led me into Ruga's private garden and through a door into a small room on the ground floor. There was a table, covered with tablets and a wall cabinet stuffed with rolls of parchment. Justus closed the door, turned and leaned against it.

'It can't be you.' He shook his head. 'It can't be.'

'It is me. I look a little different, that's all.'

'A *little*?'

Justus stared. Then his shoulders relaxed, and I saw that boyish smile tugging at the corners of his mouth.

'I didn't think I was ever going to see you again. I should have known you'd come back to check on me. Make sure I was doing everything properly. I don't know where to start. Where have you *been*, Dido? What happened to… to your hair?'

'They wouldn't have let me race in the Circus if they thought I was a girl, would they?'

'You're a *charioteer*?'

I nodded, enjoying the look on his face. 'For the Blues, I'm afraid. I always dreamed of racing for the Greens one day. Now I suppose we're on opposite sides.'

Justus sank on to the chair behind the table.

'I don't understand. It doesn't make sense. Just tell me, Dido. What *happened*?'

'Didn't your uncle tell you?'

I watched him closely for a reaction. I thought I saw guilt in his eyes, but he shook his head.

'I never believed what they said about Antonius. At least... I didn't want to. I always liked your father, Dido. Besides, as I said to my uncle, the blame shouldn't have fallen on you too. It wasn't as though you did anything wrong.'

I opened my hand hiding the berry I'd taken from the feed store and put it on the table in front of him.

'The only thing I did wrong was to find one of these in Nessus's stable that night. The only thing my father did wrong was to talk to your uncle about it. It got him killed.'

Even in the dull light from the oil lamp on the table, I could see the colour leave Justus's face.

'Antonius is dead? Uncle Ruga...?'

'No. Macro's the one who killed him. I'd be dead too, if I hadn't managed to get away.

Justus picked up the red berry, rolling it between his fingers. I studied his face and felt disappointment.

'You knew about this, didn't you?'

'Not back then. Not back then, Dido, I swear it.'

'But you know that's how the Greens are winning their races now.'

'I'm sorry. I've told my uncle it's wrong. But he's not himself. He's not been right since that night you and Antonius disappeared. I've tried to help him run things. Then, when Emperor Tiberius died and Caligula succeeded him, everything changed. Charicles deals with the ephedron, he's the one who knows how it works on horses. But it's Macro who's really in charge of the faction now. I just manage the accounts and go to races in place of Uncle Ruga.'

'Couldn't you have said something about what was going on? To one of the other faction leaders, anyone?'

'I could have done. But you don't know Caligula. He can change from one mood to another in a moment. I was afraid of what he might do… to my uncle… to me, if I'm honest. The Greens have always been the faction of the people. The whole city is drunk on their favourite team winning all the time. I'd have stirred up more trouble than it was worth.'

He ran his hands through his hair.

'I don't know what to say, Dido. I'm sorry. If I'd known it was Macro who did this to you, I'd never have…'

He stopped.

'Never what?'

'Nothing,' he muttered. 'It doesn't matter.'

The distant whine of music from the party over

our heads filled the silence between us. He gazed at me and I could tell he was comparing me to the Dido he used to know.

'I thought about you a lot, you know. What made you come back?'

'The chance to race in the Circus. I thought as well, maybe I might get to see Porcellus again.' *And you*, I thought, though that didn't seem worth mentioning any more.

'Porcellus? Oh, you mean Incitatus.'

'No, I don't. He's *my* horse, I should know his name. Whose idea was it to call him Incitatus anyway?'

'The emperor's. He's obsessed with the horse, he treats him like a pet. Even eats his dinner outside his stable sometimes.'

'I need to see him, Justus. You have to help me.'

Justus shook his head.

'I'm not sure Porcellus would know you after this long, Dido.'

'Of course he would, don't be stupid.'

'You don't understand. Charicles gives him something. To keep him sedated between races. He's unmanageable otherwise. When you stopped coming to see him, he kicked his stable to pieces. That's why it had to be made of marble. He'll break anything else.'

I felt rage but also relief. Porcellus hadn't heard my voice. That's why he hadn't come to the stable door earlier. It wasn't that he had forgotten me.

I leaned forward, resting my knuckles on the table.

'Listen to me, Justus. I was in that race today, the one where Darius's horse collapsed. It was just like Nessus, you remember that day when he went mad and almost died? Whatever's in that little red fruit might make those horses run faster, but it also does something awful to them. It kills them in the end. I heard Charicles and Macro talking about it this evening. I'm not letting that happen to Porcellus.'

'You don't need to worry about that. Incitatus doesn't get ephedron. Charicles tried it on him but it turned him so mad he almost killed one of the grooms.'

'His name's *not* Incitatus, it's Porcellus, and if you think—'

A girl's voice in the corridor outside made us both jump.

'Justus? Justus, where are you?'

Justus swore and went towards the door, but it had already opened. A young woman came in. She was sixteen or seventeen, I guessed, with cinnamon-brown curls framing a pretty, fine-boned face. The skirt of her pink dress made a rustling noise as she walked.

'Oh.' She looked at me disparagingly. 'I didn't know you were busy.'

'I'm writing a letter. This boy's waiting to take it for me.'

'You're always working. The emperor is asking for you. We're about to start dinner.'

'I'll be there soon, Ennia, I promise.'

'But…'

'Just a few more moments.'

'Very well. But you have to give me a kiss to make up for being late.'

There was an excruciating pause. I looked at the wall and tried not to listen. When she had gone, Justus closed the door and rested his forehead on it for a moment.

'Dido, you have to go.'

'Who was that?' I asked.

'The girl I'm engaged to,' he muttered.

He went to the table and scribbled a few lines on a scrap of papyrus while I absorbed the shock of what he had said. *Justus? Engaged? To that girl?*

'Here.' He handed me the note. 'Take this, go out of the side entrance. If anyone asks, you can say you're delivering it for me.'

Whatever else I felt, I was determined not to let him get rid of me without securing a promise.

'Swear you'll try and find a way for me to see Porcellus,' I said. 'You can get a message to me at the Blues' club-house. Ask for Leon, that's my name now.'

'I'll try and think of something. Just go for now, Dido. Please go.'

XXXIII

It was early but the city was already wide awake, ready for another day of games. As the wagons taking the drivers from the club-houses to the Circus snaked in procession through the different neighbourhoods, you could tell which faction each district supported from the coloured banners stretched between the buildings. Most were green, and here the residents sang rude songs as we went past. But there were a few cheers too from Blues' supporters, and their children reached up and tried to touch any part of us they could through the sides of the wagon.

I sat between Antigonus and Parmenion, both of whom were quiet. They'd been out until late last night and I guessed they had sore heads. It had been six days since I escaped the club-house and I hadn't dared risk it again. Every day, I'd gone to train with the other charioteers at the Trigarium, hoping that there would be a message from Justus on my return. But no word came. I wondered if I'd been wrong to trust him. Maybe I'd always imagined we were better friends than we were. I tried to forget the silly romantic daydreams I'd once had about him.

'How did you get that?' I asked Antigonus, noticing a bruise on the underside of his jaw.

'We ran into Nicias last night,' said Parmenion when Antigonus didn't reply. 'He was in a tavern on Stable Street. Holding court like he was the emperor himself.'

'Did you speak to him?'

'We might have had a conversation for old time's sake.'

I looked at Antigonus, who remained silent.

'Nicias said something about Anna,' said Parmenion in a low voice. 'It got ugly. Antigonus managed to land a good hit, though.'

'What about you?' I asked. 'You were the one who used to be friends with him.'

Parmenion shrugged.

'I don't know. He was always saying how he was a better driver than me, always bragging that he'd get to the Circus first. Hard to argue with him but it got to me sometimes. What I wouldn't give to have a decent team of horses and take him on now.'

As we rounded the next corner, we caught up with a crowd of supporters heading to the Circus early, trying to get good seats. Some of them carried cushions and picnic baskets. My stomach swooped.

'What is it?' asked Parmenion.

I turned, trying to find the face I thought I'd seen. But whoever it was had vanished. *It couldn't have been him*, I told myself. *He's dead. Probably it's someone who looked like him.* But the rest of the way to the Circus, I couldn't shake off the strange feeling that I had just seen a ghost.

Crito had told us the running order at breakfast that morning. Icarus, Hannibal, Mago, Perdix and I were in the seventh race. It would be their first time in the Circus and I was both excited and terrified.

'Good luck today, you four,' I said, checking that the stable boys had done a good job of grooming them. 'Make me proud. And Scorpus too.'

Icarus looked out over the door of his stall, ears pricked and eyes wide as he took in the sights and sounds – of sweating horses being rubbed down, wheelwrights arguing over repairs and stewards trying to locate missing teams. I tied his plaits in myself – as I always did for my teams now – before giving him his apple, kissing him and going to sit in the faction pit with the other drivers.

The Circus was packed as usual, every seat taken. An argument broke out behind us as a Blues supporter returned from a cookshop outside, his hands full of snacks and drinks, to find someone else sitting in his place. Musicians and dancers entertained the crowd between races. High on the opposite side of the track where most of the Green followers were sitting, there was a colourful crowd in the emperor's viewing box. The Greens dominated the first three events. To my surprise, Fabius appeared in the two-horse race, where the factions normally put their least experienced drivers. He won but looked furious and drove off the track before he could be awarded the laurel wreath of victory.

'Punishment,' said Helix, who was next to me. 'For sharing the glory with you the other day.'

In the fourth race, Antigonus drove brilliantly and for a while had a chance of challenging the Green driver for the win. Then one of our own water boys got in Snowy's way, and in swerving to avoid him, Antigonus lost the lead to the Green driver behind him.

'Damn it. That was unlucky,' said Helix. 'Same thing happened to me a few races back. Crito needs to give those lads a talking to, they're supposed to stay up on the channel.'

Just before midday, a trumpet sounded, and a procession entered the arena. At the head was Caligula himself. My heart leaped when I saw that the lone horse pulling his chariot was Porcellus. The crowd stood to applaud. Caligula wore a long green tunic and a helmet decorated with peacock feathers. I watched Porcellus closely. He was snatching at his head and it looked as if he was wearing a curb-bit to give Caligula more control. Even so, there had to be surprising strength in the emperor's thin arms. Helpless jealousy crept through me. *He's my horse, not yours*, I thought, as Caligula smugly accepted the acclaim of the Circus.

A strange prize-giving ceremony followed, despite the fact that there had been no race. As Caligula was presented with the laurel wreath of victory, an official tried to place a jewelled collar around Porcellus's neck. He reared suddenly, knocking the official over and tipping Caligula out of the chariot. A ripple went through the Circus and I watched apprehensively as the emperor picked himself up off the sand and approached Porcellus, who was now being held by six Praetorians. But after shaking a finger as if telling off a naughty child, Caligula patted his flank and waved to the appreciative crowd.

'Come on,' said Helix. 'You're on next and I'm after you.'

Reluctantly, I went with him, raging at the image of the horse I loved being paraded like an animal on a leash. As we passed the Green quarter of the forum, I saw Ennia emerging from a curtained litter. She wore a dress of pale green silk with bands over the shoulder that gave glimpses of her pearly skin. Her hair curled around her lovely face in tight ringlets. Helix noticed me looking at her.

'So, that's the kind of thing you like, is it?' He poked me in the ribs. 'Don't blame you. Pretty girl. Fabius had a thing for her, when he first joined the Greens. But don't get your hopes up, lad. She's already spoken for. Has a powerful father too.'

He pointed and I saw Macro approaching her, his brawny arms swinging by his sides. He took Ennia's hand and helped her down, patiently waiting as she smoothed a crease out of her skirt before leading her towards the Circus. I saw Justus waiting for them by a staircase.

I stared at the three of them. Voices hissed in my ear, whispering of betrayal and vengeance. They grew louder and angrier as I watched Macro rest his hand on Justus's shoulder in the way a father might show affection to his son.

'Come on,' said Helix. 'Only thing is to get out there and race. Show her what she's missing.'

Two laps to go.

The Blue section of the crowd was screaming. I ducked as a piece of debris flew past my head. Something about my mood seemed to have passed along the reins to my horses. Icarus, Hannibal, Mago and Perdix were obeying my every command as though their lives depended on it. Icarus above all seemed to understand what was at stake, curling around the corners like an eel, almost licking the posts as he went. We were third and gaining ground on the Red chariot ahead.

Behind me, I heard a crash. I was tempted to look but thought of Scorpus's words. *Ignore others' misfortunes. Race your own race.*

The Red driver was within range now. His team were clearly flagging, and I dropped the reins.

'Go, go!'

We forced our way down the narrow gap he'd left on his inside, Perdix bravely shouldering off the Red rope horse. The Blue spectators bayed their appreciation. I could taste the excitement in the atmosphere.

Just over one lap left. The Green chariot in front had about a six-length advantage. Images of Ennia and Justus and Macro kept running through my head. I shook out my whip and cracked it above my team's heads.

'Come on!'

All four responded, pushing out their chests as their hooves pummelled the sand. The Green driver didn't seem to be pushing his team very hard and we gained ground with every stride. As the final dolphin plummeted, we were on his tail. Everyone in the Green pit was waving their arms at their lead driver on the track. He glanced back and I had the pleasure of seeing the surprise on his face. Frantically, he started to lash his horses.

We raced each other along the straight, the screaming of the crowd hurting my ears. To my left, the Green driver was still cracking his whip, over and over. I cursed myself for not stealing the inside line off him on the turn. As we approached the final post, I hugged as close to my opponent's chariot as I could without our wheels touching. We came out only half a head down. Icarus's nose crept forward, as though he was sniffing victory. Twenty lengths to go. Ten. Five. The finish line marked in the sand flashed beneath us.

The Green driver and I looked at each other.

Then we looked at the official beside the track.

He hesitated. Then he raised a blue flag.

As my shoulders sagged with exhaustion, I saw the section of the crowd seated behind Otho's box stand as one.

I held my arm up in the air as I'd seen Fabius and other winning charioteers do. Icarus's ears pointed forward, as though he knew the result too.

We did it, Papa. We did it.

XXXIV

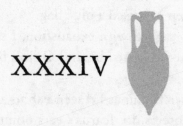

Someone pressed a drinking cup into my hand. People were taking it in turns to slap me on the back and shout things that I couldn't hear. The tavern was packed wall-to-wall with Blues' supporters, singing faction songs. Parmenion came up to me, his eyes glazed with wine.

'You did it, man-girl,' he bellowed in my ear. 'You did it.'

Luckily, it was so noisy that no one heard him. Amid the singing, people were talking loudly about my race, reliving every lap and arguing over where I had won it. I felt dizzy. My teammates kept bringing me drinks from the bar and I had to secretly pour some of them away so that I didn't lose my head completely. Fighting through the crowd, I eventually found Antigonus, leaning against a wall. He raised his cup to me.

'You should be celebrating too,' I said, my words

slurring a little. 'You would have won if that stupid water boy hadn't got in your way.'

Antigonus shrugged.

'There'll be other races. You deserved the glory today. Scorpus would be proud of you.'

I felt a tap on the shoulder. The tavern-keeper was beckoning to me.

'Someone out the back wants to talk to you,' he said, jerking his thumb towards a curtain behind him. 'Too shy to come inside.'

'Who is it?'

'Didn't give his name. Just said you'd know him.'

A warning voice fought to make itself heard above the reckless chatter in my head. I was already breaking Scorpus's rule about leaving the club-house. Glancing at Antigonus, who was now talking to another charioteer, I thought about asking him to come with me. Then it occurred to me who it might be.

The alleyway at the rear of the tavern looked deserted. There was a foul smell from a latrine, and a couple of dogs were investigating a shed that must be some kind of food storage. I was about to go back inside when a figure stepped out of the shadows.

'Why the secrecy?' I asked. 'Afraid someone will see you in the enemy camp?'

'You're not the enemy,' said Justus quietly.

'What do you want?'

'To say "well done", partly. That was a great race you drove today.'

'Thank you. That's quite the compliment, coming from the man who's going to marry Macro's daughter.'

Justus shifted his feet.

'I'm sorry, Dido. I should have told you.'

'Don't worry about it. Not worth mentioning.'

'I'm not in love with her. Ennia's a nice girl. But I wouldn't have considered getting engaged to her if Macro hadn't suggested it. I thought maybe it would help my uncle. Give me more influence at the faction.'

'Really? So tell me, when are you planning to use that influence? Any time soon? Because it looked to me today as if you were quite looking forward to being the son-in-law of a cheat and a murderer.'

'I told you, I didn't know about that! In the name of the gods, Dido, do you think that if I had, I would have…' Justus ran a hand through his hair and took a deep breath. 'I didn't come here to talk about my marriage. I came here to tell you to be careful. Caligula's furious that you won that race today.'

'Good. Hopefully it'll teach him he doesn't get his own way all the time.'

'No, you don't understand. You don't know what he's like when he doesn't get what he wants. He loses his mind… he hurts people.'

'I know. I'm the one without a father, remember?'

Too late, I remembered that Justus didn't have one either.

'Look,' I said, rubbing the sides of my forehead, which were starting to throb. 'I know you're trying to help. But everything you've said makes me want to beat them even more. Do you know what it was like for me, seeing Caligula driving *my* horse today? It's killing me, not being able to show Porcellus I'm here, to tell him that I didn't abandon him.'

Justus shook his head.

'I've been trying to think of a way for you to see him, Dido, but it's impossible. He's under guard the entire time, the emperor won't even let him graze out on the Field with the other horses. I'm sorry.'

The elation of the day had turned to despair.

'Was there anything else?'

'I suppose not.'

'Then you should go. You wouldn't want Ennia to know where you've been, would you?'

He looked at me reproachfully.

'Promise me you'll be careful, Dido. Please? Do you promise?'

He waited until I nodded. I watched him trudge away, the urge to call after him growing with every step he took.

'It's good advice he's giving you, Dido. A shame he doesn't know how bad you are at keeping your promises.'

I swung round. Cassius Chaerea emerged from behind the shed, his blue eyes bright with anger.

XXXV

I opened my eyes and saw spots of silver. I realised I was looking up into the night sky. The sound of rushing water filled my ears and my head pounded. I couldn't separate my hands and something was tugging at my feet. I struggled to get up and saw that I was lying on the back of a wagon. Cassius was binding my ankles together with rope.

'Please,' I croaked. 'I haven't put you in danger. No one knows who I am.'

'Not yet, perhaps.' Cassius yanked viciously at the rope. 'But they will eventually. Your old friend Nicias is bound to figure it out one day.'

'He won't, I promise. I've been careful, I—'

'You call being in a tavern in the middle of Rome *careful*?' Cassius dragged me upright. '*I* knew it was you the moment I saw you in the Circus today. It's quite a thing, watching you drive, Dido. Not something you easily forget.'

He lifted me off the wagon. We were on the Field of Mars, in a deserted corner of the huge plain. The dirty smell filling my nostrils was coming from the Tiber, which rushed past at an alarming pace.

'Why are we here?' I asked, my heart thudding.

Cassius didn't answer. Carrying me towards the river, he set me on the bank. Then he went back to the wagon and took an object from it, lugging it with both hands. I saw that it was a heavy weight, the kind you use for measuring grain.

'Please, no, no, no.' I tried to crawl away on my knees and elbows.

'Stop crying,' spat Cassius savagely, pinning me down. 'You think this is pleasant for me? You think I like doing this? It's your own fault, you stupid girl. I told you not to come back, didn't I? I risked my life to help you.'

'I'm sorry, I'm sorry. I had to see him, I had to.'

'See who?' Cassius was trying to tie the weight to the rope around my feet.

'Porcellus,' I sobbed.

'Who in the name of the gods is Porcellus?'

'My horse.'

Cassius paused and looked at me in disbelief.

'You came back to Rome to see a *horse*?'

I nodded, the tears pooling under my chin and soaking through the neck of my tunic.

'It doesn't matter now. I've lost him. Caligula and Macro have taken him, just like they took my father.'

I gazed into the dark swirling water. What would it be like to drown? At least I'd be with Papa again, that was some comfort. I tried to picture him, his smiling face waiting for me on the other side of the river as the ferryman's boat drew nearer. Maybe Mama would be there too. Then I realised Cassius was staring at me, the rope slack in his hands.

'Are you trying to tell me… this horse of yours… you're talking about *Incitatus*?'

'Yes. But that's not his name. His name's Porcellus. My father bought him for me. It was Ruga's money, I suppose. But I'm the one who trained him. I'm the one who saw how great he could be. But he doesn't know me now. I tried talking to him, but he couldn't hear me.'

'When was this?'

'When I sneaked into the Greens' stables a few nights ago.' Suddenly, I was laughing. It was surprisingly easy to flip from feeling terrified to light-headed.

'So Incitatus belongs to you. How interesting…'

'If you help me get him back, I'll do anything you want. Anything, I swear.'

223

Cassius held up the rope tied to my feet.

'I don't think you're in a position to bargain, Dido, do you?'

'Why didn't you kill me when Macro ordered you to? You could have done.'

'Yes, I could have. But if it was helpful to Caligula that you were dead, I'll admit, Dido, I found it satisfying to keep you alive.'

I stared at him, the breeze from the river chilling my wet cheeks. Cassius spoke softly.

'Yes, that's why I spared you. It was one thing to guard the life of a man as weak and damaged as Tiberius. It's another to perform the same office for a tyrant with the mind of an infant and the appetite of a cannibal. I'd do anything to give him a taste of the humiliation he inflicts on others.'

Cassius's eyes narrowed, his cold gaze fixed on the boiling surface of the river. It felt as if he was talking to someone else, not to me.

'You *can* humiliate him! If I keep winning, if the Greens start to lose and the Blues start to win, the people will be angry.' I was tripping over my words, knowing that I was bargaining for my life. 'The emperor won't be as popular. He'll hate that.'

'You've become rather big-headed, my girl. You've only won one race.'

'But I'll keep winning. I'm the only person

who can beat Nicias.' In my desperation, I was willing to say anything to persuade him, even if I wasn't sure I believed it. 'I know I can do it, I used to train with him, remember? And I know Porcellus... Incitatus... better than anyone. I can do it.'

Cassius was silent. I could see I had made him think.

'Let me prove it to you,' I begged. 'Please.'

'You're a good charioteer, Dido, I'll give you that. Maybe as good as Nicias, maybe better. But that roan of yours is no match for Incitatus and Otho doesn't have anything else in his stables capable of beating him.'

'Then help me get Porcellus away from them. I swear, if I could have him back, I'd leave Rome tonight and never return.'

'That would spoil your promise to defeat the Greens though, wouldn't it?'

There was no sound except the churning of the river.

'Perhaps you're right, Dido,' said Cassius unexpectedly. 'Perhaps you can help me. You win another race... and we'll see. But let us be very clear with each other. If you want to stay alive, you have to win and you have to keep winning. And if anyone suspects who you really are, then you had better start running, because I'll be after you, and there won't be anything you can say that will save you.'

XXXVI

I nailed the circle of green laurel on to the door of Icarus's stall. Icarus was greedily eating his supper in the corner and showed no interest in what I was doing.

'So this is where you're hiding.'

Antigonus was behind me.

'Not hiding,' I said, returning to my task.

'Hanging your spoils, then.'

'It's not mine. It's for Icarus.'

We leaned over the door, watching Icarus as he munched happily on his hay.

'Three wins in three races. Helix says no other Blues' driver has had a start like it in years. Most of them take at least ten or fifteen races until they get their first victory.'

'You had a good day today. Second place.'

'Only because you started the rout. Helix thinks you've set a rat in the Greens' coop. They're running scared.'

'So are their horses,' I said quietly.

'Yes, that was strange, seeing two of theirs fall like that.'

Not strange, I wanted to say. Horrible. How long would it be before people understood what was going on? The image of those horses being dragged off the track was haunting me. Their sagging jaws, their foam-streaked hides, their eyes wide with fear. If that was what ephedron could do to them, what about the effect of whatever Charicles was giving Porcellus?

'Come on,' said Antigonus. 'You're wanted in the club-house.'

Inside, the brightly painted hallways of the upper floors were crowded with people. My teammates were playing drinking and gambling games in the alcoves. Girls in thin dresses sat on the knees of elderly men. The place reeked of sour wine and vomit. I wanted to get out of there. But Otho was beckoning to me from a corner, where he was talking to a man with liver-spotted skin.

'Here he is, the new hero of the Circus!' His gold rings dug into me as he gripped my shoulder. 'Leon, I want you to meet my friend Betucius Barus, one of the Blues' most important investors.'

Betucius Barus cleared his throat.

'We must not get ahead of ourselves, Otho,

calling this boy a hero. The Greens are still winning most of their races.'

'The tide's turning, though, Betucius,' said Otho triumphantly. 'Leon here is putting fear in the Green camp.'

'He hasn't been properly tested yet. That's only going to happen when you put him up against Incitatus.'

'Let's give the boy time to build his reputation.'

'Just as I thought,' said Betucius with a knowing shake of his head. 'You don't think he can win. Does anyone?'

Otho looked annoyed. Helvia swirled up and draped her fingers over his wrist.

'Senator Valerius is saying his farewells. You should see him out.'

She smiled at me. 'The man of the hour,' she murmured as she led Otho away.

Betucius abandoned me without a word. Gratefully, I seized the chance to escape. But near the door, someone stepped in front of me. I almost yelped.

'I wanted to offer my congratulations,' said Cassius Chaerea, holding up his cup in salute. 'A splendid victory today.'

He drank, watching me over the rim of the cup as I tried and failed to meet his intense gaze with defiance. Someone jostled us and Cassius put his hand on my arm.

'Rather crowded, isn't it?' he said. 'Might I tempt you to join me out here?'

His grip tightened and I understood it was an order, not an invitation. Heart thumping, I followed him, passing a loud group of dice players which included Parmenion and a plump girl with blue eyelids. There was a small red room off the hallway, lined with cabinets. Cassius stepped aside ushering me ahead and then, after checking the hallway, pushed the door shut.

'You're certainly getting better at keeping your promises, Dido.'

'Why are you here?'

'I told you. I'm a lifelong Blues supporter. They know me well on the club-house gate.'

He strolled about, studying the old charioteers' tunics in the cabinets on the walls.

'Your victories are having the desired effect, Dido.'

'What do you mean?'

'The emperor is rattled. Last night, he said he couldn't sleep because of the noise of people lining up outside the Circus to secure free seats for today's games. He ordered the palace guards out with clubs to beat them to a pulp. Word has flown through the streets. Caligula's star is starting to wane, even with his own faction's supporters. So it's very, very important, Dido, that you keep winning, as we agreed. Do you understand?'

'If the Green horses keep dying, it might not matter what I do. When is someone going to care about what's going on?'

'It's easy for people to shut their eyes against things they don't want to see. Between you and me, though, our friend Macro looks like a hunted man. Just as I suspected, he promised the emperor unlimited victories. Now he is failing to live up to that promise.'

Cassius paused by a side table and picked up a bronze inkpot shaped like a chariot. Idly, he started to play with it.

'Have you spoken to your friend Justus recently, Dido?'

'No.'

'He seemed concerned for you that night I surprised you. I felt as if I was interrupting a lovers' assignation.'

'We're not… it's not like that.'

A faint, not unsympathetic smile creased the lines around his eyes.

'But you did love him once, didn't you, Dido? What a pity. Never mind, hearts mend quickly when you're young. We'll just have to hope you can trust your friend not to give you away.'

'I can trust him.'

'That's a big gamble to make when your life is at stake, isn't it?'

'Yours too.'

I said it without thinking. The mockery in Cassius' eyes vanished.

'Don't threaten me, Dido. I can make you disappear any time I want to. Remember?'

He waited until I nodded, then set down the inkpot and left the door swinging as he went. Trembling, I stared hopelessly at the tunics in the cabinets. Cassius said I had to keep winning. But there was only one way that this could end. It wasn't just Betucius who didn't believe I could win against Nicias. Icarus was a good horse, but Porcellus was a great one. Nicias would win – in my heart I knew he would. Macro's worth to Caligula would be restored and I would have broken my promise to Cassius yet again. The thought of running now, of finding a boat that could take me back to Utica, was tempting. But if I went back there, Cassius would know where to find me. And he would kill me for sure.

A soft swishing interrupted my thoughts and I turned. Helvia was standing in the doorway, watching me.

'Good evening. I hope I'm not disturbing you.'

The hem of her violet silk skirt brushed the floor as she came to stand beside me, bringing a warm fragrance of roses into the room. She was close enough for me to see the brush-strokes in her thick white make-up.

'Quite extraordinary, aren't they?' she mused as she inspected the faded blue tunics. 'Like ghosts trapped in this little box. To think of the adoration they once inspired. I must admit, I find it such a childish passion in many ways. If it were the swiftness of the horses or the skill of the drivers that the supporters really cared about, I could understand it. But it's a piece of cloth that captivates them. A piece of cloth on whose colour their entire happiness depends.'

Her grey eyes studied me. Then she put out a hand and gently stroked my cheek with her manicured finger.

'Quite extraordinary,' she repeated.

In a swirl of silk, she drifted out of the room.

XXXVII

'Race eight! Race eight! Chariots ready!'

The mood in the changing room was different. The Blues' charioteers were used to the occasional voice wishing them good luck as they left – now they departed to shouts of encouragement from all sides. The plunge pool was full of jubilant drivers, reliving their races, talking about how close they had come to winning on the last corner. I could sense the change in the Red and White quarters too. In the distance, the Circus rumbled like an angry mountain.

Crito appeared with a tablet in his hand.

'It's going well, boys. Watch out for that crowd of Greens by the south corner. Their aim's pretty good today.' He consulted his tablet. 'Four races to go. Leon, you ready?'

I nodded and he leaned over the bench where I was sitting.

'I mean it about being careful today,' he said. 'Watch yourself. The Greens are looking too cocky for my liking. Feels as if they might have something planned. Keep an eye out for any trouble, you hear me? Good lad.' He straightened up and scowled. 'Parmenion, get that girl out of here.'

Parmenion, who was in the corner of the changing room, nose to nose with the girl with blue eyelids, didn't seem to hear him.

I headed off to check on my team. There was a big cheer from the Blues' supporters as I emerged from the changing room and a crowd followed me over to the stalls, held back only by the rope that separated them from the horses. In his stall, Perdix was objecting strongly to having blue ribbons tied into his tail. Hannibal and Mago were placidly munching hay while their coats were brushed. I went over to Icarus, who was having his feet checked. He was sweating a little more than usual but otherwise his ears were pricked and his brown eyes brightened when he saw me.

'Good boy.'

I rubbed him behind his ears and slipped him a piece of apple. A boy sitting on his father's shoulders at the back of the watching crowd was waving, trying to catch my attention. I smiled and gave him a little salute, which made him wobble with joy.

A man in a threadbare cloak was standing next to the boy's father. He had his hood pulled up, which seemed odd on such a hot day. I could just see his face under uneven brown stubble. Something about the way he was gazing at me so intently made me stare back.

Eager supporters tried to grab me as I pushed into the middle of the crowd. I fought them off, tearing my arms from their clawed grasp. When I reached the spot where the man had been standing, there was no sign of him. The boy who had waved at me from his father's shoulders was speechless in the belief that I had come over to talk to him.

'Where did he go?'

Father and son looked puzzled. I scoured the sea of heads. The forum was packed with faction hands, race supporters, street traders. A movement caught my eye. Someone running, a cloak billowing behind.

I headed in pursuit, trying to keep sight of the man through the crowd. A trader swore as I knocked some tunics off his cart. I kept going, swerving around people as if I was racing in the Circus. But when I reached the other side of the forum, I lost sight of him. I was about to ask a woman carrying a basket if she had seen anyone when I noticed faint ripples in a puddle and wet footprints leading into a side street.

Cautiously, I edged along the street. I could hear snatches of conversation from the windows, caught the smell of cooking. A mangy dog trotted past, snuffling at my ankles. At the far end of the street was a huge pile of rubbish. Otherwise it was a dead end. I turned on the spot. He had to be here.

'Come out,' I called. 'Please. I know it's you.'

The banners over my head flapped gently in the breeze. Nothing else moved. I tried again.

'Please. Come out. I have to see you.'

There was a tiny noise from a doorway in shadow. A dark shape slowly peeled away from the wall.

The person inside the cloak peered at me. For all that I'd been so sure, I couldn't believe my eyes. It really was him. But how could it be? He was dead, Cassius had said so.

'*Atticus?*'

XXXVIII

I gazed into the face of Papa's old friend as he pushed back the hood of his cloak. His cheeks, once plump and smooth, were hollow and lined. Matted hair curled over his shoulders.

'I don't understand. You're supposed to be dead.'

'Could say the same of you, Dido.'

Atticus's chuckle turned into a coughing fit that bent him double. He hit himself in the chest until he stopped wheezing.

'Not used to running that hard. Leg's still pretty sore from where those Praetorians beat it.'

'They threw you into the river. Macro's men. Someone told me.'

'True enough. Tied a weight to my ankles to make sure I went down. But you don't survive being shipwrecked in the Circus as many times as I did without knowing how to slip a rope. I was quite the escape artist. Your father used to call me…'

His face crumpled and he began to cry.

'I'm sorry, Dido. I'm so, so sorry.'

Someone in a room high above us yelled at him to shut up.

'It wasn't your fault,' I said eventually.

'It was, Dido. Don't try to pretend that both of us don't know it. If I hadn't done what Ruga said, if I'd told Antonius what was going on in the first place, none of it would have happened.' Another coughing fit left him helpless. 'I... had to run just now. I didn't think you could ever forgive me.'

He clutched my hand, his watery eyes squinting at me.

'Couldn't believe it when I saw you the first time. Thought it must be my eyes playing tricks on me. What are you doing, racing for the enemy, hey?' He tugged playfully on my blue sleeve.

'You recognised me? How?'

'Saw you in a race. Thought it was Antonius, come back to life. Crouched low like that, holding the whip just so. Then I saw your horse's mane. I thought to myself, no one except Dido plaits like that.' He started coughing again.

'What happened to you, Atticus? Where have you been all this time?'

'Soon as I got out of that river, I made myself scarce for a while. Couple of friends gave me a place to sleep. Been living on the streets for the past year or so though. Quarto, the cook from our old clubhouse, lets me have scraps of food from time to time. Can't resist coming for a race day. Long as I keep my head down, none of the Green crowd recognise me. They all think I was helping Antonius to cheat by drugging horses. I should have told everyone what happened but I was afraid those Praetorians would come after me.'

He looked guilty.

'I tried to find you, Dido, really I did. I looked in every corner of the city I could think of. Where did you go?'

'Do you remember a charioteer called Scorpus? From your and Papa's day?'

'Scorpus of the Blues?'

'That's him. When I ran away that night, I hid on a boat and it took me to Carthage. I thought maybe I could find some of my mother's family, but when I got there, I found Scorpus. He told me Grandfather Muttumbaal was dead. So he took me in and taught me how to drive and that's how I ended up here.'

In the distance, I could hear someone shouting for Leon. It was one of the grooms. They must be about to call my race.

'Atticus, there's no time to explain more now. We can talk again after…'

It was only then that I noticed Atticus was trembling. I thought he was about to start coughing again but his hands were shaking as he raked them through his hair.

'Atticus? Are you all right?'

'I just can't believe it. Never thought I'd hear that name again.'

'Who?'

'Scorpus. For you to run into him. Of all people.'

His words stirred a memory. That was exactly what Cassius Chaerea had said. *Of all people.*

'Papa told me about the two of them. But he still thought Scorpus was a great driver. If he was willing to put it behind him, why shouldn't I?'

'He was a forgiving man, your father. If it had been me, I'm not sure I could have done the same.'

'Well, it's all in the past now. Atticus, they're calling my race. I have to go. I'll come and find you afterwards. Wait here for me.'

I set off down the street.

'She was a beautiful woman, your mother. Kind too.'

His unexpected statement made me turn back.

'My mother?'

'Never saw two people more in love than her and Antonius. Scorpus said he was sorry, did he? About the accident?'

'Whose accident?'

'Your mother's, of course.'

'What's Scorpus got to do with Mama's accident?'
Atticus looked startled.

'You don't know? But I thought you said you did?'

'Know what? Atticus, just tell me what you're talking about.'

'No. Antonius always made me promise never to talk about it in front of you.' He had started to shake his head and rub his hands together. 'He never wanted you to know.'

I was terribly afraid now.

'They were so happy before he came along. Then he turned up and tried everything he could to tear them apart.'

'I don't understand. Was Scorpus...' I wrestled with an uncomfortable thought. 'Was Scorpus in love with my mother?'

Atticus stared at me.

'But... you mean... you don't even...? How could he? How could you have been with him all this time and he didn't even tell you?'

'Tell me what?' I almost shouted.

'He's your own blood, Dido. He's Sophonisba's brother. Your uncle.'

In the distance, someone kept calling for Leon.

Feeling dizzy, I put my hand against the wall to stop myself from toppling over. It couldn't be true. It couldn't be. But somehow, I knew that it was. Atticus was muttering.

'I'm not saying he caused it. The accident, I mean. She'd done that trick a thousand times... but whatever Scorpus said to her, it broke her heart and took her mind away from where it should have been. She'd never have fallen otherwise. After it happened, there was nothing on his face. Not a tear, no grief, nothing. Antonius was out there in the middle of the track, trying to breathe life into her. Not Scorpus. He just walked away.'

'Why didn't they tell me?' I whispered. 'Why didn't either of them tell me?'

Atticus looked stricken.

'Dido. I'm sorry. I thought you knew, I thought...'

Blindly, I made my way back to the forum. By the warm-up circle, Parmenion was talking to one of the Blues' engineers who was shaking his head and shrugging. Icarus, Hannibal, Mago and Perdix were being trotted up and down by a groom.

'Where have you been?' demanded Parmenion as soon as he saw me. 'Everyone's been looking for you, they're about to draw lanes.' He looked closely at me. 'Are you all right?'

I took the reins of my chariot from the groom. Icarus tossed his head in the air. I knew the lack of a proper warm-up had unsettled him and cursed my own foolishness. As Parmenion and I drove towards the steward next to the urn, I saw Justus standing in the faction owner's area beside the warm-up circle. He stepped up to the fence as I came closer, an urgent look in his eyes as though he wanted to speak to me. I was about to pull on Icarus's reins when a delicate hand appeared on Justus's shoulder.

'Come on, dearest,' I heard Ennia say. 'Papa's kept seats for us in the emperor's box.'

I turned away as Parmenion came alongside.

'It's our old friends again.' Parmenion nodded and I saw that Darius and Scylax were waiting in the line-up. 'Better watch it, Dido. I don't like the look on their faces.'

I remembered Crito's warning.

They loaded us into the start gates. I had drawn one of the middle lanes. As I waited for the countdown, hearing the chanting of the crowd getting louder as they worked themselves into a frenzy, I felt the walls of the tiny cell closing in on me. A voice in my head screamed the same question over and over again. *Why didn't you tell me, Scorpus? Why? Why?*

Five. Four. Three. Two. One.

XXXIX

Icarus's ears went up the way they always did. He loved being in the middle of the pack, tearing out of the gates. But there was a churning in the pit of my stomach. Something was telling me to pull up, but I couldn't think clearly through the swarm of thoughts raging in my head. Thousands of Blues' supporters were already standing in their seats.

'Icarus! Icarus!' they chanted. These days, they could almost match the Green supporters in volume.

We took the first corner, the whole field keeping close together. I usually didn't like being the front runner, but Parmenion's suspicions and Crito's warning had unsettled me. Seeing Darius and Scylax closing in from either side, I switched tactics. The Blues cheered as we took the lead from one of the White chariots. Urging my team into a gallop, we quickly left the field behind. I felt as if I was running away from a pack of Furies.

As we turned for the start of the second lap, I heard thundering hooves behind us. Perdix snorted in delighted welcome as his friend Snowy came up alongside him.

'They're right on our tail,' shouted Parmenion.

We completed the lap, Parmenion keeping level with me, both of us aware of Darius and Scylax just behind. I knew we couldn't keep such a fast pace for another five laps and, as the second dolphin dropped, I tried to ease on the reins, thinking I would go to the back for a lap or two instead. But Darius blocked my path, covering every escape route. Parmenion and I both took our teams wide at the next turn, hugging the outside of the track, leaving plenty of room for more chariots to drive through. But no one would take the bait. The White and Red chariots were happy to let us use up our teams' strength.

Parmenion pointed to the track ahead.

'I'll try and get them to follow me!'

Snowy and his teammates flattened their ears and accelerated at Parmenion's command. One of the Red chariots went with them. Icarus wanted to catch up with Snowy, but I held him back. Glancing behind, I could see that Darius and Scylax were hunting me, like a pair of vultures.

The third dolphin plunged. We were almost at the half-way point in the race and Parmenion was leading, with me in third. The Blues' supporters were in full voice. As I passed our pit, I saw Antigonus alongside Helix, their hands cupped around their mouths. Crito was in his usual spot at the front. He clenched his fist at me in a gesture of encouragement.

On the fourth lap, Darius drove up on my inside. I left plenty of room for him to come past, confident in Icarus and Perdix's finishing speed. But instead of overtaking, he turned his horses sharply to the right, ramming my chariot, then doing it again a second and a third time. The impact sent jolts of pain through my whole body as I fought to stay on my feet. I suspected an ambush and looked for Scylax in case they were planning to attack me from either side. But he was a few lengths back.

We were nearing Parmenion and the Red chariot. The fast early pace had tired their teams. As the fifth dolphin dived, we came out of the first turn almost neck and neck in a line of four. I looked across at Darius, expecting him to stop playing games now and attempt to take control of the race. But he wasn't looking at the track ahead. He was still concentrating on angling his chariot into mine. Our wheels made contact. I gritted my teeth.

It was then that I noticed the foam on Icarus's coat. A thick white crest spreading from his shoulder to his neck. I heaved on the reins in terror, desperate to pull up as quickly as I could. Darius's wheel clashed again with mine, making me lose my grip. As I steadied myself, I could hear someone yelling above the screams of the crowd. Parmenion was on my other side, waving his arms. I shook my head, unable to make out what he was saying. He started pointing frantically. I glanced down and at that moment, the base of my chariot gave way.

My helmet was torn off as I smashed into the Circus floor. Everything went black. I tasted sand and blood and I was struggling to breathe. My skin felt as if it was being ripped off. The reins tethering me to my outside horses was pulled taut like a noose around my waist. My team were bolting, terrified of the broken chariot shaft dragging behind them and of the screaming crowd. The reins cut even deeper into my torso; I couldn't get my breath.

Someone was shouting. *Your knife.* I grabbed at the front of my leather breastplate, trying to pull the knife from its pocket. I almost had my hand on it when something blocked out the sun. Scylax's team of bays were almost on top of me. I could see the sinewy undersides of their heads and feel the sand being kicked on to my ankles. Scylax himself was peering over the side of his chariot, lining up his horses like an executioner aiming his blade.

I kicked and twisted, fighting to keep my flailing legs out of harm's way. My fingers closed on the hilt of the knife. Wildly, I slashed at the reins above my head. The pressure around my waist lessened slightly. I sucked in a gulp of air before it tightened again. I hadn't cut the rein cleanly. My right foot grazed the hard wall of the channel. We were running dangerously close. Above me I could see the heads of the water boys leaning from their posts, their expressions dark and blank against the bright sky.

I screamed in agony. One of Scylax's horses had trodden on me, its weight sending pain surging through my leg. Then I saw a moving shadow as Parmenion leaped across from his chariot into Scylax's. The bay horses swerved to one side. Parmenion and Scylax grappled with each other, struggling to stay upright. Summoning all my strength, I hacked at the frayed rein above my head. It gave with a snap and I felt my bones crunch as my body slammed into the track, tumbling into darkness.

When I opened my eyes, Antigonus was kneeling over me. The blinding sunlight behind him made me squint.

'Where is he... where's...?'

'It's all right. There's help coming.'

Turning my head with difficulty, I saw men with stretchers running towards us. A group peeled off to where two people were lying in the sand next to the wreckage of a chariot.

'Parmenion,' I said, trying to raise my head. 'Is he...?'

'No. He took a bad spill but he's alive. Lie down.'

The pain was like fire, spreading intense heat through my body. It struck me how quiet it was. Usually there was a buzz among the spectators at the Circus whenever there was an accident. But I could only hear a faint murmur and a whining noise rising above it all, like a fly flitting next to my ear.

'Where are the horses?' I asked Antigonus.

'You'll see them afterwards. Don't talk.'

Ignoring the stretcher carriers' attempts to get me to lie still, I pushed myself up on to my elbow. Hannibal and Mago were being led away from the ruins of my shattered chariot further down the track.

'What about Perdix and Icarus?'

'Just don't move.'

Something in his voice scared me. Now I realised what the noise in my ear was. A child was wailing. Crying its heart out. I squinted harder. Antigonus tried to block my view but I'd already seen it. Perdix was standing alone by the finish line, a long, broken rein trailing from his harness. A dark shape lay on the ground next to him.

'No.'

'It's all right... Leon... stop...'

I started to crawl along the track on my elbows. The stretcher carriers tried to hold me back, but I tore myself from their grasp and hobbled as fast as I could. They caught up with me just before I reached him. As I was wrestled to the ground, the vet standing beside Icarus laid a blanket over him, covering the horrible smear of white foam on his beautiful blue roan coat.

XL

In the end they had to bind my arms and legs to the stretcher in order to carry me out, which was agony after the flaying they'd taken from the arena floor. They took me to a cell under the Circus. The floor was stained with blood and there were gruesome metal instruments on the walls. Antigonus stayed with me. I begged him to tell the stewards that I had to see Icarus.

'Maybe there's something… maybe he's still alive… can you go and see if he's breathing… maybe there's a way…?'

He put his hand gently over my mouth. My body heaved, my sobs stifled by his palm.

They carried Parmenion in afterwards and put him next to me. His leg was a mess of blood and broken flesh, and his eyes were half-open. When two more stretcher-carriers tried to bring in Scylax, Antigonus snarled that they should take him elsewhere. After a brief argument, they left.

The Circus physician came in. I tensed as he started to prod my arms, legs and ribs. I had bandaged my chest that morning, but if he looked too closely he was bound to discover the truth. Antigonus looked wary too. Luckily, the physician made his diagnosis quickly.

'No broken bones. Some bruising to the ankle. Usual treatment,' he said to his assistant. 'Pig's dung for the lacerations to the skin. Thyme and opium for the pain.' He moved on to Parmenion. 'This one wasn't so lucky. We can probably save the leg but he's going to need a splint and something to get him drunk while we set the bone.'

'Yes, please. Make me very drunk,' muttered Parmenion.

'It'll still hurt worse than you can imagine,' said the physician. 'You won't race again for a while.' He glanced at the door of the cell where a shadow had appeared.

'Charicles, your man's next door. Don't like his chances of keeping that arm.'

I tried to free myself from the ropes tying me to the stretcher.

'I know you,' I shouted, as the watchful, hollow-cheeked face of Charicles retreated into the dimly lit corridor. 'I know what you did. You killed him! It was you! You killed him…'

Antigonus put his hand over my mouth again, pressing hard. The physician said something about my having taken a knock to the head. Groans of pain were coming from the next-door cell. The physician went out and voices floated through from the corridor.

'... very good of you to come, Master Justus. The emperor asked me to see what was happening.'

'How is he, Charicles?'

'They're probably going to have to take his arm off, I'm afraid. The chariot smashed to pieces against the channel when that lunatic jumped into it.'

'Macro wants you back at the stables. I'll see that Scylax is looked after. You can—'

Awful screams obliterated their words. I looked at the metal instruments on the walls and closed my eyes.

Justus came into the cell and closed the door quickly.

'Get out,' I hissed.

Justus didn't move, looking warily at Antigonus and Parmenion.

'They know about me,' I said. 'They're my friends. I used to think you were too.'

'Dido, I swear I didn't know what was going to happen.'

'Yes, you did. I saw it in your face at the warm-up.'

'Who *is* this?' asked Parmenion faintly.

'I knew they were planning something,' said Justus in a low voice, as Scylax's agonised screams continued, 'but I didn't know what. I heard Charicles and Macro talking. They said something about the emperor being in a better mood once your race was over. I wanted to talk to you, to tell you to drop out.'

'Well, you can tell your girlfriend's father that if it's the last thing I do, I—'

'There must have been someone who knew from our side too.'

Antigonus was holding something between his finger and thumb. It looked like a splinter of wood, but we could see it was soft when Antigonus rubbed it between his fingers.

'I looked at your chariot before we came off the track,' he said to me. 'Someone put wax pins in your axle. That's why the wheels came away so easily. Anything could have happened out there on the track. But no one could have done this to one of our chariots unless they were inside our camp.'

We all stared at the shard of wax between Antigonus's fingers. Scylax's screams had turned to groans.

'Justus? Are you down here?'

The door opened. An old man stood there. He had white hair and although he was tall, he stooped badly. As he came into the light from the single oil lamp in the cell, I was startled to see that the thick eyebrows, which had once been a wolfish grey, were now white too.

'I'm coming, Uncle Ruga. You should have waited for me at the top of the stairs, like I told you to.'

'Oh dear. Is one of ours hurt?'

He came into the cell, his body shaking as he clutched a stick for support. Justus went to him and took his arm. It was like watching a parent with an infant taking their first steps.

'You've taken a knock, haven't you?' he said to Parmenion, peering at his bloodied leg. 'Never mind. You'll be back holding the reins again soon, winning races for the Greens.'

Parmenion gave Antigonus and me a look out of the corner of his eye as if to say, who's this old fool?

Ruga sniffed the air.

'I know that smell. Pig dung. I remember it from when Lepidus... do you remember, Lepidus, Justus... no, before your time. One of the worst shipwrecks I've ever seen. Antonius didn't think that he would survive. But...'

Ruga frowned, the wisps of his brows touching in the middle. He seemed confused, as if a thought had gone missing in his head and he was trying to find it again. He bent over me, staring through tired, fearful eyes. For a moment, I thought I saw a glint of recognition in their cloudy depths.

'I'm sorry,' he said, his voice trembling. 'I'm so sorry you were hurt. I never would have put you in any danger…'

'Come now, Uncle,' said Justus quietly. 'We have to go.'

He led Ruga to the door and pushed him through it. Glancing back, his eyes met mine. Then he was gone.

XLI

I lay in Icarus's empty stall, staring at the shadows cast by the oil lamp. The straw was banked in deep furrows. Icarus used to kick it with his feet, like a child playing in puddles. Some of the hay he'd been eating earlier was still in the trough. He always liked to save a little for when he came back. I had already found a tell-tale red berry, buried deep in the pile.

A stable hand came to clean the stall, but he left when he saw me. They'd wanted to keep me in the club-house sanatorium overnight. Helix had visited me there and told me the story of when he was first shipwrecked. 'It's all good practice for the next time. You're not a charioteer until you've been wrecked a few times. You'll get over it, lad. Sorry about your little roan. There'll be other horses.'

Parmenion was asleep in the sanatorium. I'd had to watch him suffer the operation by the

Circus physician. When it was done and he was left sweating and white-faced, I waited until the physician had gone and then stroked his forehead until he stopped shaking.

'You getting sweet on me now, man-girl?' he asked, his teeth chattering.

'No. But thank you. For what you did out there.'

'I'm sorry it didn't help Icarus.'

'It was my fault. I should have seen something was wrong with him before the race. He'd suffered so much because of me. First Nicias. Now this.'

Parmenion squeezed my hand as I started to cry.

'That horse knew more love than he ever would have done his whole life because of you. He loved racing and he died with the wind in his ears and the whole Circus Maximus chanting his name. Wouldn't mind going that way myself.' He shut his eyes and sucked air through his teeth. 'Especially the way this bloody leg hurts.'

We lay there for a long time in that dark cell under the Circus, like two children shivering in a cold wind.

The rain was pelting down. Savagely, I hoped that it was soaking the Green supporters who were no doubt celebrating Icarus's death. Then I heard the click of the latch on the door. Probably that groom again. Or maybe it was Cassius, coming to punish me for breaking my promise. Whatever I had coming, I felt I deserved. The door of the stall creaked open. Someone stood on the threshold, rain dripping down their head. A tall, familiar figure. He didn't say anything as I climbed out of the straw, the shock of seeing him numbing the pain of my torn skin. He looked wary but sympathetic. I could see the grey stubble on his cheeks where he hadn't shaved.

'Dido, stop it. What's the matter with you?'

Scorpus tried to grab my fists but I snatched them from his grasp, thumping him anywhere I could. I managed to land one good punch on his chest before I slipped and fell. My head suddenly felt too heavy to lift. The words echoed through my mind and I couldn't stop myself saying them.

'He's gone,' I gasped. 'He's gone.'

'I know. I know what happened, Dido. I just got here.'

I knocked his hand away as he attempted to hold mine.

'Don't try and tell me you're sorry. You never cared if he was hurt. You used that cruel bit on him.'

'I know what he meant to you. I'd feel the same if I lost Sciron. Which I didn't, thanks to you, and I'll never forget it.'

'What are you doing here?'

'I heard a rumour at the market in Carthage. That the Blues were winning again, and it was all because of this new driver called Leon.' Scorpus smiled. 'I had to see it for myself. Came straight to the Circus as soon as I reached the city. I was in time to see Nicias in the last race. Otho told me about Icarus. I'm sorry. It was madness for me to let you put yourself in danger like that. You could have been killed.'

'It wasn't your decision and don't talk to me as though you're my father. Not after what you did.'

I got to my feet and limped into the rain, every step hurting.

'Where are you going? Wait, Dido…'

'Why didn't you tell me?' I screamed, the words feeling as though they were ripped from inside me. 'Why? Why didn't you tell me?'

I saw that he understood. Any hope I'd had that Atticus might have been confused or mistaken drained away.

'Dido, wait. Let me explain.'

'There's nothing to explain. Go away. Leave me alone, you coward.'

'I am a coward. I admit it.'

'So, what? You want a reward?'

'At least let me tell you now.'

'How long were you planning to wait before you revealed your big secret? That you and I are *family*! That it's your fault my mother died!'

'Yes, it was my fault!' He was shouting now too. 'That's why I couldn't tell you because every single day for the past fourteen years, I've had to live with that! How could I admit it to you, you of all people?'

We glared at each other through the pounding rain.

'Look, just come inside, where we can talk. We'll drown if we stay here.'

'I don't care.'

'How did you find out?'

'What does it matter? Atticus told me.'

'Atticus? I thought he was dead.'

'Well, he's not.'

Water pooled around our feet from an overflowing drinking trough. Scorpus rubbed his eyes.

'Your mother and I...' He stopped and started again. 'Your mother and I were very close as children. We were the nearest in age and we always loved each other the best. I used to let her come with me on the practice chariot when I was helping my father. I can still remember how hard she laughed. She used to beg me to go faster. I made that model of Tigris you're wearing for her. She had a magical way with horses. I remember her playing on the straw in the stalls when she was small. Our mother worried that the horses would trample her. But they treated her as if she was one of their own, even the fiercest beast in my father's stable.'

The faint smile of memory on his face faded as quickly as it had appeared.

'Then she got older and she fought against learning a woman's work. My father forbade her to drive with me. When she turned fifteen, he told Sophonisba it was time for her to marry and learn to be a wife and mother. He had chosen a friend of his to be her husband. Just before the wedding, Sophonisba ran away. None of us knew where she had gone. My father told us never to mention her name. I didn't know if I'd ever see her again.'

'Two years later, a scout came by and bought me to drive for the Blues. To race at the Circus Maximus was my greatest dream come true. I came to Rome and on my first day at the track, I saw Sophonisba. At first, it was just like we were children again. She was so happy to see me. I was so relieved she was safe. But I had become too much my father's son. The idea of her doing what she was doing – performing on horseback in front of all those people – seemed shameful. I told her she had to stop, that I would take her home if she didn't obey me. That's when I found out about her and your father. You were only a few months old. I became obsessed with beating Antonius. I convinced myself that if I could humiliate him on the track, I would win back Sophonisba's loyalty.'

He paused. I waited, afraid of what was coming.

'On the day it happened, there was a big race with a big prize at stake. Antonius and I were leading on the final lap. Usually we respected each other enough to race fairly, but some Fury possessed me that day. I tried to shipwreck him. Antonius managed to hold me off and he won. As soon as we got out of the arena, we went for each other. If it wasn't for Sophonisba getting between us, one of us would probably have ended up dead. I told her she had to choose – Antonius's love or mine. She was beside herself, pleading with me. Then they called her into the Circus. Her team always finished their act with the same trick. They would gallop seven horses in a row, each rider standing astride two horses, before they all jumped a flaming fence at the same time. I'd seen Sophonisba do it any number of times before. If I'm honest, I was proud of how brave she was. Only this time, she was obviously thinking about other things. She slipped and fell. The track hadn't been raked. Her neck broke as she hit the sand. I knew it was my fault as soon as it happened. But I couldn't say it, to Antonius or anyone else.'

Scorpus wiped his eyes. The rain was starting to ease.

'Next day, I left Rome and went back home. When I told my father what had happened, he said it was the gods' way of punishing Sophonisba for dishonouring him. I never spoke to him again. Glarus sold me some land and I set up my own stable with the prize money I'd won at the Circus. A year later, I married Ayzebel. She was kind and gentle and she made me a better man. But the guilt I felt over Sophonisba never left me.'

For the first time since he'd started talking, he looked me in the eye.

'That's why I didn't want you to come here, Dido. I didn't want to lose you the way I lost Sophonisba. I won't force you. I'll never make that mistake again. But I owe it to Antonius. I owe it to him to do everything I can to keep you safe.' He laughed bitterly. 'Though I suppose you're going to tell me he'd have let you stay and drive.'

'No,' I admitted. 'He didn't like me racing either.'

I noticed for the first time how the shape of his face was just like mine. How could I never have seen it before?

'I'm not going back,' I said. 'Not until I've made Macro and Caligula pay for what they did to Icarus and to my father.'

'Revenge will eat you from the inside, Dido. Look what it did to me.'

Someone was approaching us from the direction of the club-house. It was Antigonus.

'So you are here,' he said to Scorpus. 'Otho said he saw you. What are you both standing in the rain for? Come inside.'

'I'm not staying,' said Scorpus. 'I want Dido to leave with me tonight. You can come too, if you want, and Parmenion. I heard about his accident. There's a ship leaving Rome for Utica. Anna would be pleased if you came home.'

'Don't use her to try to get me on your side. If you want to help, then stay here. We need you, Scorpus. Otho's just got rid of Crito.'

He nodded at me.

'It was him, Dido. He put the pin in your chariot. He's been in their pay all this time. That's why our water boys kept sabotaging their own drivers. It was Otho's wife who suspected him. She got her slave-girl to follow him this evening. Saw him in a tavern in the Green quarter, taking a hand-out from Macro.'

'That was for Icarus. I'm going to kill him!'

'Enough of this,' said Scorpus. 'You two don't know what you're getting yourselves into, these are dangerous people you're trying to—'

But Antigonus cut across him.

'Just come to the club-house and talk to Otho. He wants to see you.'

XLII

A slave-girl admitted us into Otho and Helvia's private dining quarters at the top of the club-house. It was a luxurious room with thick crimson rugs and hunting scenes from a forest painted on the walls. Helvia was lying on a silken couch, a pink peach in her hand. Otho was hunched over a low table covered with the remains of their dinner. He was furiously shelling nuts.

'Bloody Crito,' I heard him growling as we entered. 'First Fabius, now him. They all follow the money. What happened to loyalty?'

'A little less heat, my dear,' said Helvia. 'We have guests.'

'Ah, Scorpus, good, you're back. It's Fate that's brought you here tonight.' He jabbed meaningfully with his finger. 'Now we'll have them! You can take over from that traitor Crito and get this place in order. We'll buy some new horses, find a new team for Leon here...'

'Don't get ahead of yourself, Otho,' said Scorpus.

'But you've got to help me! You're my last hope, everyone else has abandoned me, curse their hides.' He threw a walnut across the room. Helvia winced as it left a mark on the wall.

'My dear, where are your manners? Scorpus, come and join us. Corinna will fetch you a plate.'

'Thank you, I'm not hungry.'

'Well, at least sit down.' She smiled and beckoned to Antigonus and I, standing just outside, unsure what to do. 'Yes, you may come in.'

Otho leaned forward, elbows resting on his knees.

'Help out an old friend, Scorpus.'

'From everything I've already seen and heard, there's nothing I can do for you. Face it, Otho. Either accept the way the dice fall or get out of the game.'

'It's not going to be my choice, if you don't help me! The other backers want me to sell them my share in the faction. Betucius is leading them, damn his ugly face.'

Helvia took another bite of her peach.

'Perhaps you need to start a new game, Otho,' she said in her sleepy voice. 'One where you make the rules.'

Otho frowned. 'What do you mean?'

'Why don't you make the Greens an offer? A special race between Rome's two favourite teams, the Greens and the Blues, with a special prize.'

'What sort of prize?'

'Fifty million sesterces, let's say. Both factions put up half the stake. Winner takes all.'

There was a long silence. Otho blinked at his wife.

'Are you trying to ruin me, Helvia? Fifty million sesterces?' He turned to Scorpus. 'This is why they don't put women in charge of things. No head for business. My dear, do you realise that if I lost half of fifty million sesterces, I'd be finished? I'd have to leave Rome, start up my business somewhere else.'

'It will probably come to that, anyway.'

'Oh, and you'd be happy with that, would you? No more shopping for you, my dear. No more of your jewels and fine dinners.'

'You would find a way to start again, Otho. You always do.'

Otho tapped a finger against his wine cup.

'The crowd would love it, that's for certain. And that sort of money would be enough to bring us about for a time.'

'At least we know the odds will be a little fairer now that Crito won't be drugging our horses and meddling with our chariots,' said Helvia. She looked speculatively at Scorpus. 'What would it take?'

'To beat those black horses I saw Nicias driving today?' Scorpus shook his head. 'I've only ever seen one team that could equal them, and someone here sold them.' He looked accusingly at Otho.

'What, the Four Winds? I told you, Crito said they were past it.'

'*Crito* said. Has it occurred to you, Otho, that the reason they lost their form was because Crito did something to make them lose it?'

Otho turned red and waved his hands as if he was trying to get rid of a fly.

'Well, it doesn't matter anyway. They're gone, no way of getting them back. Crito sold them on for me. I didn't ask where they went.'

'Lucky my sources are more reliable than yours, then.'

Otho straightened up.

'*What?* Do you mean to say you know where they are?'

I could tell that Scorpus was regretting having said anything.

'Well,' he said, after a pause, 'there was no way I was going to let horse-flesh like that go to rot without at least trying to track them down. Not after all the work I put into them.'

'Well? Where are they?' demanded Otho.

'Glarus took some of his boys to compete at the

games in Leptis Magna. He found Eurus and Auster there, racing as a pair. I'd told him about you selling them and he was a good enough friend to buy them back for me.'

Otho leaped off the couch.

'I knew the gods themselves had sent you to me!'

'Don't get excited, Otho,' said Scorpus firmly. 'I've put the word out, but no one's seen Zephyr or Boreas anywhere. Without those two, you haven't got a four.'

'I've got some good horses here…'

'Forget it. That rope horse Nicias was driving today might well be the best I've ever seen. But the Four Winds were the perfect team and the perfect team is what you need.'

While Otho and Scorpus continued to argue, I stared out of the window. It made me proud to hear Scorpus praising Porcellus. But something was nagging at me, like a worm burrowing inside my head. I peered down the hole it had created and found myself back outside the club-house gate on that warm night before my first race as I returned from visiting the river. A horse with a straggly mane and leather blinkers stood by the open door to the Blues' yard. It lashed out at the man holding its rope, kicking him hard in the ribs.

'What if we could find them all?'

Everyone turned towards me.

'What do you mean, Leon?' asked Helvia.

'I'm sorry. I was asking Scorpus. What if we could find all of the Four Winds? Could we win?'

'Why do you ask?'

'I think I know where Boreas is.'

Otho practically threw himself on his knees in front of me.

'*Where?*'

'He's pulling a grain cart. I saw him on the street outside on my second night here. He looked so different, I didn't realise it was him until you started talking just now.'

Otho leaped to his feet and started doing a little dance, clapping his hands.

'Calm down, Otho,' said Helvia. 'Scorpus? Does this change things?'

Scorpus frowned at me and I knew what he was thinking. *Why couldn't you keep your mouth shut?*

'I'll believe it when I see it and even if it's true, we still don't know about Zephyr. He's the most important member of the team.'

'But what if we did?' pressed Helvia. 'What if we could find him? Would you help us?'

Scorpus chewed the inside of his cheek.

'They haven't raced as a team for the best part of a year. I don't know if I'd be able to get them back to the way they were. If I could, well... maybe. But if the Greens find out it's the Four Winds they're up against, they might not take your bet.'

'Then we'll need to give them a reason to believe that they will win,' said Helvia.

'What do you have in mind?'

Helvia smiled and waved her fan gently.

'A mystery charioteer.'

Otho's face brightened.

'Of course! Scorpus! Why didn't I think of that? You could drive any of those Green charioteers into the ground!'

'You've got to be joking, Otho. I'm ten years too old for it.'

'I wasn't thinking of Scorpus, as a matter of fact,' said Helvia apologetically. 'His reputation goes before him. The Greens wouldn't consider him weak enough opposition.'

'So who were you thinking of, then?'

'Just what I said. Someone they believe they can beat. Someone... or rather something... the Circus Maximus has never seen before.'

Her eyes came to rest on me. It was like being caught in the gaze of a hungry-eyed predator.

'I assume *he* is in on the secret?' she asked Scorpus, nodding to Antigonus, who was standing silently by the door. 'He must be, if you trained both of them.'

'Secret? What secret?' demanded Otho.

'I'm afraid I don't know your real name, my dear,' said Helvia, addressing me. 'But I think we should all stop pretending, don't you?'

She smiled.

'Won't you tell me your name? Please?'

'Dido,' I whispered.

'Dido. What a pretty name. You are a very brave young woman. I should love to know more about you. Come, sit here with me.'

Otho's mouth had fallen open. He stared as I reluctantly went and sat on the couch next to Helvia.

'Do you mean to tell me…?'

His eyes roved over my face, travelling down my body before coming to rest on my chest.

'Don't be crude, Otho,' said Helvia, an edge to her voice.

'But… this is impossible! Are you telling me that's a *girl*? Scorpus?' Otho rounded on him. 'Did you know about this?'

'Dido, don't say another word,' said Scorpus.

'Why didn't any of you tell me? A female charioteer?' Otho seemed to be having trouble getting his words out. 'The Circus would have loved it. They'd have come from miles away! I could have made an absolute *fortune*!'

'Well, now's your chance, my dear,' said Helvia

calmly. 'Tell the Blues' supporters you're bringing back the Four Winds and that you've found a girl who can race.'

'No,' said Scorpus. 'It's absolutely out of the question.'

'We could make her a mysterious princess, perhaps, from some far corner of the empire,' mused Helvia. 'It would be just like something out of an ancient tale. Caligula would adore it.'

'I said no,' repeated Scorpus.

I gave him a look. 'Are we back to this again? You telling me what I can and can't do?'

There was a long silence.

'We'd still need to find Zephyr,' he said.

'I know. I've been thinking about that. There's someone who might be able to help us.'

XLIII

A cool wind had blown into the Alban Hills, making the needles whisper on the tall pine trees around Otho's country estate. We had left Rome in the middle of autumn and now the winter rains were arriving, filling up the fountains and fishponds that surrounded the enormous villa. I'd been amazed to discover that as well as stables and paddocks, there was a vast practice track. The change in the weather was turning the surface to mud, but Scorpus and I worked every day for as long as we could, until the light faded.

Mornings were all about the horses. I would exercise Eurus and Auster on the practice track while Scorpus lunged Boreas on a long rein. He'd been in a horrible state when Scorpus and I had found him, rib-thin and dirty, though with enough of the old Boreas in him to try to eat the pouch of money that Scorpus handed over to the delivery drivers. A daily diet of rich alfalfa hay and bran mixed with olive oil had restored some of his old gloss and muscle.

Eurus and Auster, who had arrived on a cargo boat from Utica before the weather turned, needed no such careful handling. A few months of being driven at a provincial circus didn't seem to have done them much harm and according to Scorpus, they were in good condition. My job, he said, was to build up their stamina so that they'd be ready for the longer distance in the Circus Maximus. I would mix medium-pace laps with fast ones, increasing the miles each day until their legs were hard with muscle. They were a dream to drive. It felt disloyal to Hannibal and Mago to say so, but I had never before driven horses who raced so well together as a pair, their movements mirroring each other's as if they were thinking the same thoughts at the same time.

In the afternoons, while the horses rested, it was my turn to be put through my paces. Scorpus made me exercise, climbing up and down the steps to the villa repeatedly until my legs shook from the effort. He gave me heavy rocks to lift above my head and hold there while he counted so slowly that I would crack and scream at him. Some days it hurt so much that I cried. But Scorpus was never sympathetic.

'You need to be strong to drive these horses. They won't look after you like your old team. They'll take direction from you as a last resort and if you don't give it, there won't be any controlling them.'

Helvia came to watch us sometimes. She'd arrived before the weather turned, saying she was bored of the city. Otho was still there, tasked with planning the upcoming race as well as explaining the disappearance of 'Leon'. I didn't much like the idea of people believing that the trauma of my accident had made me lose my nerve and return to Utica. Far more worrying was the fear of how Cassius Chaerea might react to my departure. I had nightmares of him pursuing me to the country. But when I explained my fears to Helvia before Scorpus and I left Rome, she told me to leave Cassius to her. 'The best revenge is always conjured by a woman. He will understand,' she said, her eyes glinting. Since I hadn't yet woken up to the sight of a murderous Praetorian looming over me with a knife, I had to trust that Helvia was right.

We didn't often see her before the afternoon. Occasionally, I would catch glimpses of her in her luxurious dressing room off the atrium, lounging, eyes closed, as Corinna painted her face or curled her chestnut hair. After lunch, she usually lay on a cushioned couch on the portico that ran along the front of the villa, a pitcher of rose-scented water at her elbow. From the practice track, I could sometimes see her painted fan waving like the tail of a cat.

'He pushes you very hard,' she said to me one day as I collapsed at the top of the villa steps, sweat pouring off my forehead. 'It's obvious he cares for you, though.' She continued to fan herself as I caught my breath. 'There's a resemblance between you. Should I pretend not to have noticed it?'

'He's my uncle,' I said, as soon as I was able to draw breath.

'I did wonder. Your father's brother?'

'No. My papa died.'

All of a sudden I was crying and I couldn't stop. It was the first time I had ever said those words aloud and it felt as if something inside me had burst. Helvia came and sat next to me on the top step, the edge of her green woollen mantle draping the stone like moss. With whispered encouragement from her, I told her everything: about Antonius's death, about my mother and Scorpus, Porcellus and Icarus. When my grief had exhausted itself, Helvia took out a square of linen and carefully wiped my cheeks.

'This boy you talked about. Justus. He's the young man who's going to marry Macro's daughter, isn't he?'

I nodded.

'I'm sure he felt everything for you that you did for him. But we often grow out of our first love.'

She pushed a few strands of hair back from my forehead, tucking them behind my ear. It was strange how comforting it felt.

'Your hair is getting longer. You'll need to pin it up soon.'

'I know. I can't decide how I prefer it. I've been Leon for so long and now I'm Dido again. But when I go to the Circus, I'm going to have to pretend to be someone new. Sometimes I wonder who the real me is.'

'Oh, I think I see her clearly enough.' Helvia smiled and I noticed for the first time how warm her eyes were. 'Tell me, has Scorpus heard anything about Zephyr?'

'No. My friend, Atticus, he's gone looking for him. Atticus knows everyone in the racing world. He's going to visit all the dealers and stables he knows, see if he can find out who Crito sold him to. I don't think Scorpus thinks he will.'

'We shall have to hope. I wonder, if your friend does find Zephyr, how will you feel, racing to win against Incitatus?'

'I don't know. As if I'm betraying him in a way. I came here hoping I could get him back somehow.

But now I see it's impossible. So I have to try and win. For Papa, for Icarus… and for me too.'

I hoped she might say something, suggest some way that Porcellus and I could be together again. But she just kept stroking my hair and nothing more was said between us.

One evening, near the end of the month, Scorpus and I were leaning on the fence, watching Eurus, Auster and Boreas swish their tails as they grazed in the twilight. Eurus was nibbling Auster's neck. Suddenly his head came up and Auster's did too. I listened.

'Did you—?'

Scorpus put a finger to his lips, telling me to be quiet. There it was again. A horse, screeching a greeting from somewhere across the valley. Now Boreas's head lifted. His nostrils flared, his eyes widened. Then they were off, all three of them, cantering to the other side of the field, pushing their chests against the fence. Scorpus and I hurried to the main gate of the villa. A wagon was trundling along the sandy track from the main road. Its driver was wrapped in a thick cloak. There was a horse tethered to the back of the wagon by a long rope.

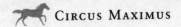

Its head came up and it neighed again. The response from Boreas, Eurus and Auster came at once in an excitable chorus.

'You found him, Atticus!' I cried. 'You found him.'

XLIV

Atticus gnawed at the pork bone as though it was the last thing he would ever eat. Helvia watched him with a mixture of curiosity and mild distaste.

'More wine?' she asked, nodding to Corinna, the only slave present, who was holding the jug.

Atticus shook his head, wiping his mouth with the back of his hand.

'No, thank you, Mistress.' He sat up straighter. 'Forgive my manners. Been a while since I ate as well as that. Last piece of meat I had was a fried rat.'

'I'm glad my cook's food compares favourably.'

Scorpus was leaning against one of the columns of the portico, watching Zephyr as he grazed with Boreas, Eurus and Auster in the field below. They were peaceful now, but their reunion earlier had been like watching a group of old friends who hadn't seen each other in years.

'What do you think?' I asked Scorpus.

'He's got some lesions on his girth.'

'Probably from a set of greaves digging into him,' said Atticus, picking meat off the pork bone. 'The dealer I bought him from said he got him in a trade with a soldier in one of the Rhine legions. Recognised him as a circus horse right away. Drove me a hard bargain. Just as well I had all that money you gave me.'

'Will he be all right?' I asked, looking between them.

'I daresay,' said Scorpus. 'Not much difference between a battlefield and the Circus Maximus.'

Atticus wiped his plate with a piece of bread. He and Scorpus still hadn't really looked at each other since he arrived.

'Would anyone care for dessert?' asked Helvia, breaking the silence.

'No, thank you,' said Scorpus. 'I'm going to go and check the fencing, it looked a little weak in the far corner. Don't want any of these animals to get loose now. Past experience has taught me the hard way.' He gave me a nod. 'You should go to bed soon, Dido. We've got a long day of training ahead tomorrow.'

He said goodnight to Helvia and left.

'You should go and talk to him,' I said to Atticus.

'Not sure there's much to say.'

'Atticus, I know about everything that's happened. I need you to go and make your peace. Just like I have.'

'If that's what you want, Dido. I know I've got to make it up to you, for what I did. Loved Antonius like a brother, would do anything to…' His voice started to waver.

'Yes, I know,' I said quickly, not wanting him to cry in front of Helvia. 'Just go and talk to him.'

Atticus got up and blew his nose.

'There's something I brought for you, Dido,' he said. 'I asked Quarto to fetch it for me, after I got out of that river. Gave it to a lady friend of mine to keep safe. She didn't much want to give it back, if I'm honest. But I know Antonius would want you to have it.'

He made an awkward bow to Helvia.

'Thank you for your most gracious hospitality, mistress. Most delicious meal.' He shuffled away.

'I believe Corinna put the mysterious item in your room for you, my dear,' said Helvia. 'You should go and get some sleep, as Scorpus said. Goodnight, Dido.'

'Goodnight.'

My room was next to Helvia's. She had insisted on moving me there when she arrived, refusing to allow me to sleep in the slaves' quarters. The walls were painted with birds and lemon trees and there was a bed with finely woven blankets and a washstand with a pitcher of water and a dish of scented oil to clean the dirt from my skin. I thought of Anna and our little room off the kitchen at Utica. She would love that oil. If I made it out of the Circus alive, I would make sure to take some back for her.

Outside, in a shaft of light from the moon, I could see Scorpus using a large hammer to ram one of the fence-posts deeper into the ground. Atticus was standing nearby, watching him. I couldn't tell if they were speaking. I closed the shutters on the window as quietly as I could.

On my bed was a small sack. The neck was tied tightly with twine. As I worked it open, I caught the faint scent of lavender. Heart pounding, I thrust my hand inside and pulled out a square of soft white material, crumpled from being squashed at the bottom of the sack. The gold thread was intact. I lifted it up to my face and breathed in deeply. My tears quickly soaked the fabric.

There was something else inside the bag. I reached in again and drew out a tiny round box. Opening it up, I found the lock of my mother's hair still inside.

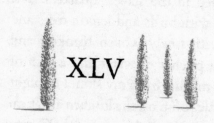

XLV

Otho arrived on a mild, damp afternoon as the clouds of winter started to lift. His litter was carried up to the villa as we were finishing a training session with the Four Winds. Thanks to Scorpus, my body was stronger than it had ever been and seeing those four chestnut heads in front of me, controlling their acceleration with just a touch of my whip, I felt like I had a god's powers. But Scorpus would never let me spend long testing their pace. He was making me do a more difficult version of the pyramid test, the wooden cones placed so closely together I had protested when I first saw them. Steering through them required every bit of strength and concentration I had.

'You're sounding like Nicias,' he remarked, when I screamed with frustration as my inside wheel made contact for what felt like the hundredth time.

'Don't compare me to him.'

'Here, come here. Pull them up. Take a deep breath. Now look at me.'

Sulkily, I met his gaze. He mimicked my expression and looked so funny that I burst out laughing. Scorpus smiled.

'That's better. Stop focusing all your effort on steering. Look where you want to go. See beyond the turn. Nicias isn't going to hand you any opportunities. So you must take your chances when they come, because there won't be many.'

On my third go after that, I did a clean run, just as Otho came out on to the portico, a drinking cup in his hand.

'Magnificent work, Scorpus,' he called out. 'They're looking like the team of old!'

'They're not quite there yet,' said Scorpus.

'Well, you haven't got much time left.'

'The race?' asked Scorpus. 'The Greens have agreed to it?'

'They have indeed,' said Otho, looking pleased with himself.

'How long have we got?'

'Come on up and eat something and I'll tell you all about it. You too, Dido.' He raised his cup to me. 'Helvia wants your company.'

We ate in the dining room, an enormous spread of roast meats, vegetables and sauces laid across a vast table. Otho and Helvia lay on couches while Scorpus and I sat opposite them. I still wasn't used to such rich food and found it hard to eat very much. After the final course of milk pudding and figs had been served, Helvia dismissed the slaves.

'So. When's it going to be?' asked Scorpus.

Otho rubbed at his teeth with a silver pick.

'Fifteen days.'

'Otho, tell me you're joking.'

'What? You've had four months to prepare, haven't you?'

'Zephyr's only been here for half of that time and Boreas still isn't completely right. Dido needs more time to get used to them.'

'Well, Caligula was very keen. Loves the whole idea, so I'm told. He's been ill over the winter. No one seems to know what was wrong with him but they were worried he might not survive it.'

'Who told you that?'

'Macro, the Praetorian Prefect, came to see me. Wanted to know all about this mystery driver – who she was, where I found her.'

'What did you tell him?' asked Scorpus sharply, exchanging a quick glance with me.

'Don't worry, don't worry.' Otho waved an impatient hand. 'I kept it all a secret. He seemed more amused than suspicious. Thinks it will be just the thing to distract the emperor. So you see, it's all set up perfectly.'

'It's too soon,' said Scorpus. 'We need more time.'

Otho's shoulders slumped.

'I can't wait any more, Scorpus. My money's almost all gone. Betucius and the other backers want me out. They're planning to hold a vote.'

Helvia rubbed his back soothingly. I looked at Scorpus, who was shaking his head.

'If I had another month…'

'I'm ready,' I said firmly.

Otho looked relieved.

'Wonderful! Wonderful! The whole city is talking about the race! Even the Red and White supporters are fired up by it. I've had posters put up everywhere and sent people to spread the word. "The Four Winds return… driven by a beautiful princess!" It's caused a fantastic stir. I think some people are expecting Helix to show up dressed as a woman.' Otho chuckled. 'I haven't even told you the funniest part. The emperor's going to host a banquet for the princess at the Greens' club-house, the night before the race.'

He looked at us expectantly.

'Otho. Tell me you didn't agree,' said Scorpus.

'Of course I did! An invitation to dine with the emperor. Can't turn that down.'

Scorpus made a gesture of appeal towards Helvia.

'You're a sensible woman. You don't think this is a good idea, do you?' he asked.

Helvia waved her fan enigmatically. Then she reached and gently encouraged me to lift my chin.

'Leave it to me. She'll be ready.'

XLVI

It was the eve of the race and I sat on a chair in Helvia's dressing room on the top floor of the Blues' club-house, my teeth tightly clenched. Corinna was poking my scalp with what felt like instruments of torture. Strands of my hair were being wrapped around a metal cylinder that glowed hot. I could see the tight ringlets as they were unwound and draped over my shoulder. They smelled like bread just out of the oven. Helvia was standing beside me, watching her slave-girl's handiwork.

'It's a shame we have to keep it dark. I'd like to see you with your own colour. The gods only know what's in that bottle of dye you showed me.'

'My friend Anna gave it to me.'

'Friend or not, it could have made your hair drop out. I knew a lady that happened to once. Poor woman. Never saw her in public again.' She tugged one of my ringlets. 'This one by her ear isn't quite right,' she said to Corinna. 'Do it again.'

'Have the Four Winds arrived yet?' I asked, trying to scratch the back of my neck.

'Keep still. No, Scorpus and Atticus are bringing them tonight. We want to make their arrival as dramatic as possible.'

Corinna stood back and waited for her mistress's approval.

'Yes, that's good,' said Helvia. 'Now for the rest.'

Corinna brought over a silver tray covered with a dizzying array of little jars and strange instruments. First, she patted white powder on to my face. Then she poked at my lids and lashes with brushes daubed in what looked like soot, making my eyes water. Helvia, meanwhile, was going through a huge chest of jewellery. She chose a gold band to encircle my upper arm and a heavy strand of amber and turquoise stones which she fastened around my neck. Fat pearls were hooked on to the newly made holes in my ears. Then she took over from Corinna, dabbing at my cheeks and lips with some kind of red paste which tasted of flowers.

'Now, stand up.'

Between them they unwound the wide piece of linen cloth which had protected my long blue tunic. I looked down at my feet. It felt strange only to be able to see my toes, which had been painted gold to match the thread on the sleeves and waist of the dress. Sandals were slipped on my feet and the strings tied for me. A blue mantle was swathed around my shoulders and Helvia showed me how to hold it off the ground. Finally, she picked up a thin gold band.

'The final touch,' she said, positioning it carefully over my hair. 'What's a princess without a diadem?'

'What if they find out I'm not one?' I asked her.

'No one really believes you're a princess, my dear. Certainly not in the emperor's circle. It's a game, something to entertain the crowd.' She smiled. 'But you look like a princess. That's all that matters. Now, let me see you properly.'

She stood back. A slow smile spread across her face. I thought for a moment that she looked sad.

'Beautiful. I always wanted to have a daughter to dress.'

'I don't feel like myself.'

'That doesn't matter, my dear. It's what others believe you to be that will count tonight. Trust me. In the Circus tomorrow, you will be yourself. Now, come along. Otho will be waiting for us downstairs with the litter.'

People were lining the streets outside the Blues' club-house. I was amazed by how many there were and how much noise they were making. Faces kept appearing in the gaps of the drapes over Otho's litter and bodies pressed against the fabric as the litter-carriers tried to squeeze through the crowd.

'My strategy worked,' said Otho proudly above the din. 'The whole city's talking about this race. They're desperate to see the charioteer princess!'

The crowds who would normally have surrounded the Greens' headquarters were being held back by nightwatchmen. There was a chorus of booing from the Green supporters which Otho acknowledged with a wave as he got out of the litter. Praetorian Guards flanked either side of the club-house gate. In front of it was Macro. I told myself to breathe.

'Otho.' Macro sounded amused. 'I should have you arrested for disturbing the public peace.' He nodded to Helvia and looked me up and down. 'So. This is your princess.'

I put my chin up, drawing strength from the hatred I felt.

'Very nice.' Macro laughed. 'I'd love to know where you found a girl this brave, Otho. This way. He's looking forward to meeting you.'

He led us down a path illuminated by torches, making small talk with Otho, while Helvia and I walked behind. I was surprised when we were taken through the gate that led into the stables, instead of into the club-house itself. The hem of my long tunic kept catching on my feet. Helvia touched my arm.

'Lift your mantle. Walk more slowly. Hold your head up,' she murmured. 'Remember what we talked about. He'll want you to act like a princess – it's part of the game. Don't behave as though you're impressed by him.'

We were led towards the sound of music and chatter. As we entered the yard between the second and third stable blocks, I saw that it was full of people, men in purple-striped tunics and women in bright dresses with their hair piled on top of their heads and jewels glittering at their throats. Couches and tables had been set around the yard, which was lit with torches, and slaves in green uniform were standing to attention with silver trays and wine-pitchers. A group of musicians were playing pipes in a corner.

Helvia's hand pressed gently into my back. I held my head high and my expression still as Justus came to meet us.

'Otho, I think you know my future son-in-law, Justus,' said Macro.

'Indeed. I see more of him than I see his uncle these days.'

'You must accept my apologies on behalf of my uncle,' said Justus. 'His health hasn't been good lately.'

Otho grunted disbelievingly and gestured behind him.

'My wife, Helvia, and this… this of course is the princess.'

Justus bowed.

'The emperor has been eagerly awaiting your arrival. Will you allow me?'

The crowd parted, their faces inquisitive and hostile. In the middle of the yard was a low table with three enormous dining couches. One of the couches was covered in gold cloth and set slightly apart from the others. It was occupied by a woman in a yellow dress and a slender man dressed all in purple.

'I don't know what game you're playing, Dido,' whispered Justus. 'But whatever you do, be careful what you say to him. Don't anger him.'

We reached the couch. Justus waited until its occupants had finished talking and acknowledged his presence.

'Emperor, may I present the Princess Sophonisba.'

XLVII

Caligula lay on the couch like a loosely coiled snake. He had a pale, babyish face and his hair lay thin and threadbare across his scalp. A loose purple robe was slipping off one bony shoulder. His bare feet were being massaged by an old man kneeling on the ground.

'How famous. How simply famous.' Caligula's voice was unexpectedly gentle. 'You'll have to excuse my not getting up to greet you properly. I am only recently recovered from illness and am still a little weak.' He patted the empty space on the couch next to him. 'Please. You are the guest of honour.'

I was surprised by his respectful tone. Then I noticed his companion hiding a smile. Trying to remember Helvia's advice, I arranged myself as elegantly as I could on the couch beside the emperor, keeping as much distance between us as I could politely manage. Caligula gestured to the woman.

'My sister, Drusilla. She has been quite as desperate to meet you as I have.'

Drusilla had the same pointed chin and small mouth as her brother. But she was much the better-looking of the two.

'How extraordinary,' she said. 'You're just like one of those women from Sparta who do gymnastics without any clothes on.'

'Don't be mischievous, Drusilla,' said Caligula, a wicked gleam in his eye. 'We don't want to make her feel uncomfortable.'

Drusilla took an olive from the bowl at her elbow and threw it at her brother. He picked it up and threw it back. They both giggled and to my astonishment, began wrestling each other on the couch. I was pushed almost to the edge as Caligula lay on top of his sister, holding her wrists until she begged him to stop, tears of laughter rolling down her cheeks. Suddenly Caligula sat up and clapped his hands.

'I'm hungry. Why don't they serve dinner?'

Almost instantly, a procession of slaves appeared with platters of food, fanning out to the tables. The guests began to arrange themselves on the couches. I could just see the bright peacock blue of Helvia's dress on the other side of the yard, as she reclined between Otho and Betucius.

'Macro, why don't you take that couch, with

Justus and your lovely daughter. Now, where is our other guest of honour?'

Caligula's eyes wandered over the crowd. 'Nicias! Nicias!' He waved like an excitable child.

Nicias detached himself from a group of Green charioteers who had been openly smirking at me. He loped towards us like a panther. His hair was long and glistening with oil and a gold chain hung around his neck. He was a man now, no longer a boy, but he had that sulky, narrow-eyed expression of his younger years.

'Nicias, my dear friend.' Caligula extended a jewelled hand to him which Nicias bent and kissed. 'I want you to meet someone. This is your beautiful challenger, who you'll be facing in the Circus tomorrow. What do you think of her? Are you intimidated?'

Nicias turned to me and our eyes met. Was that a knowing look I saw? If it was, he had his own reasons for pretending he didn't recognise me. After making a mocking bow, he collapsed carelessly on to the couch next to Macro and grabbed a handful of olives from the table. Caligula laughed.

'Neither of them giving anything away. What famous sport we're going to have tomorrow.'

He hit a golden spoon against his cup. Everyone immediately fell silent.

'My friends,' said Caligula. 'Honoured guests. What a delightful occasion. A warm welcome to all of you from the Blue faction. A special welcome of course to our *royal* guest.' Caligula took my hand in a limp clasp. 'We have all been so curious to set eyes on her. I think we can agree that if her skill with a chariot matches her beauty, then my friend Nicias has a difficult challenge ahead of him. Win or lose tomorrow, he must have already lost his heart.'

He looked teasingly at Nicias, who sucked the stone from an olive and spat it out. Caligula laughed.

'Two great factions. Two beautiful young people. I'm sure we are all looking forward to seeing them race tomorrow. In the meantime, please, eat, drink, enjoy yourselves.'

He raised his cup and the dinner began. Caligula abruptly lost interest in me. His head was never far from Drusilla's and they seemed to be laughing at some secret joke. Thankful to be spared his attentions, I took in the strange scene, the guests in their finery, the silver plates, the silent slaves, while inside the stable blocks the horses peered over their stalls, the glow from the torches reflected in their startled eyes. In the third block, only one stall's occupant was not looking out. A lone Praetorian stood guard in front of Porcellus's marble door. I locked eyes with him. Not by the slightest change in his blank expression did Cassius Chaerea betray to me what he was thinking. I glanced towards Helvia for reassurance and saw her give me a slight nod.

Justus lay on the couch opposite me, his jaw tense, eating little. Next to him, Ennia was chattering to her father. He nodded as he listened to his daughter, but he seemed to be paying more attention to the emperor, who in turn was now trying to engage Nicias in conversation. It was like watching a schoolboy in the company of one of his heroes, rather than an emperor and a charioteer.

The first course was cleared and the second brought in. Caligula tore the flesh off a small songbird, threw down the bone and burped loudly.

'I don't feel at all well.' He turned on his back, laying his head in his sister's lap while she stroked his stomach. 'Where is Charicles with my tonic?'

'We'll send someone to fetch it,' said Macro. He motioned to a slave standing nearby. Caligula sat up. His eyes were sparkling.

'No. I want Cassius to fetch it.'

He leaned over the back of the couch.

'Cassius? Oh, Cassius? Could you come here, please?'

Cassius left his post and approached the emperor's couch. He didn't look at me.

'Cassius, where is Charicles?' asked Caligula.

Cassius bent down and said something quietly in the emperor's ear.

'My ears are still rather blocked, I'm afraid,' said Caligula loudly. 'Could you speak up, Cassius? I didn't quite hear you.'

Cassius cleared his throat.

'He's in the feed store, Emperor.'

'In the *feed* store, did you say?' The emperor's voice had suddenly risen in pitch. Drusilla snorted with laughter.

'Yes, Emperor.'

'I see. In the *feed* store,' squeaked Caligula. 'Fetch him for me, Cassius, now there's a good little girl.'

Drusilla screeched with laughter. The other guests at the table soon joined in. It was obvious they were used to hearing this impersonation and that they also understood how they were expected to react.

I glanced at Cassius. His expression hadn't changed but his jaw was set and I remembered what he'd said to me that night by the river. *I'd do anything to give him a taste of the humiliation he inflicts on others.*

Caligula pursed his lips, like a baby.

'Oh, don't look like that, Cassius. It's unkind of me to make fun of you, I know. Still, I can't help wondering if you don't believe that guarding a horse isn't just a *little*' – Caligula's voice squeaked again – 'bit beneath you.'

'It is an honour to guard so magnificent an animal, Emperor.'

'Very good. A politician's answer.' Caligula pointed his toe playfully at the old man who was kneeling on the floor, massaging his feet. 'Probably the sort of answer you should have given, Senator, when I asked you what you thought of my reforms.'

The man nodded but said nothing, continuing to rub the emperor's feet.

Caligula moved so fast that I jumped. Seizing the old man by the neck, he forced his face into the remains of a bowl of walnut sauce on the table.

'I didn't quite hear you, Senator. What was that you said?'

The man gurgled, the sound of sauce being sucked into his nose and throat.

'No. Try again. I almost heard you that time.'

Caligula was snarling like a dog, his hollow eyes opened wide. None of the guests at our table moved or said a word. I thought they were all going to watch silently as the man choked to death. The emperor's grip slackened. His victim came up for air, coughing and vomiting the sauce. Caligula lay back on the couch, picked up a speckled quail's egg and started to peel it.

'You were saying?'

'Yes… yes, Emperor,' the man sobbed. 'I should have been… more respectful.'

Caligula beamed and popped the egg into his mouth. The whole yard was quiet now. Cassius Chaerea's blue eyes met mine. He bent over the emperor's couch.

'Perhaps the princess would like to meet Incitatus, Emperor?'

Caligula sat up.

'Yes! Yes, Cassius, what a good idea!'

He grabbed my wrist, picking an apple from the table with his other hand. I felt everyone's eyes on us as Caligula dragged me over to the stable block and down the path between the stalls. He unlatched the door to Porcellus's marble cell. Macro appeared suddenly at Caligula's side and put his hand on the door, keeping it shut.

'I'm not sure that's wise, Emperor.'

Caligula turned his pale eyes on him.

'Why not?'

'Incitatus will be excitable ahead of the race tomorrow. You know how he is when Charicles hasn't been in to… soothe him. I think you should leave him be.'

'Are you telling me what to do again?' Caligula's voice was gentle. But I could recognise the danger signs now, as well as Macro could. He took his hand off the door.

'No, my emperor. Of course not.'

Caligula opened the door and clutched my hand.

'Give us more light,' he commanded Cassius, who picked up a nearby torch and raised it.

Shadows woke in the corners of Porcellus's stall. It was even bigger than it looked from the outside, as spacious and beautifully decorated as Helvia and Otho's dining room. There was a mural of a black horse painted on one wall and a water trough below it made of what appeared to be ivory. Porcellus was standing in the corner, facing away from us. He wore a purple head collar, secured by a long rope to a metal ring on the wall. Caligula made a kissing noise.

'Hello, Incitatus. Come on, baby. Come and see Daddy.'

Porcellus watched Caligula out of the side of his eye as he approached. I knew that look. Under different circumstances, I would have warned anyone going near him to keep their distance.

Caligula held out the apple. Porcellus didn't move.

'Come on now, baby. See what Daddy's brought for you!'

He dropped the apple as Porcellus struck quicker than a snake, the edge of his hoof just missing the emperor's head. Caligula stepped back but Porcellus was in a frenzy, pulling against his rope, squealing with rage. He reared, almost hitting his head on the rafters. Some of the mortar holding the metal ring to the wall broke away. Macro came in, dagger drawn.

'No,' shrieked Caligula, 'don't touch him.'

I clicked my tongue.

Porcellus dropped down and became completely still. He stared at me, head up, eyes wide. I made the noise again. His ears stood rigidly to attention.

'There. There now,' I said. 'What's all this?' I went to him slowly, and gently rubbed his neck. It was damp with sweat. Still Porcellus didn't move. It was as if he had been turned into a statue. I put my nose to his neck. The feel of his soft pelt against my cheek brought a hard lump to my throat. 'There now. It's all right.'

'I was told I was needed…?'

Charicles was standing in the doorway, obvious annoyance turning to amazement as he stared at Porcellus and me. Caligula was also watching us. His expression was unreadable.

'Do you need me, Emperor?' asked Charicles.

'I don't feel well,' said Caligula finally. 'I want to go home. Charicles, bring my tonic to the palace.'

He marched out of the stable and I heard him screaming at someone. Only Macro and I were left inside the stall with Porcellus.

'How did you get that horse to do that?'

Macro's brows were drawn together in a frown. I tried to walk past him, but he grabbed my arm. There was a snap as the rope attached to Porcellus's collar suddenly pulled taut.

'Who are you? Where did Otho find you?'

I looked down at his fingers biting into my flesh and then into his brutish face. There was a thin line of sweat around his hairline and a strange reek about him. *You're afraid*, I thought with vicious satisfaction.

'The princess's litter is waiting, Macro. The banquet is over.'

Justus was standing next to Cassius. Macro released my arm and I forced myself to ignore the sound of Porcellus becoming hysterical at my departure. As I walked past Cassius, out of the stable block, I saw the ghost of a satisfied smile on his lips.

XLVIII

The door to the Circus changing room opened. Otho came in and quickly slammed it on the noise of the Forum and the faces of supporters clamouring outside. A few strands of his oil-slicked hair were sticking up and he was out of breath. Scorpus was applying chalk to my hands to give me a better grip on the reins.

'Is she ready?'

'Almost,' said Scorpus. The sound of his hand slapping mine echoed around the changing room.

'I met a group of supporters outside who told me they walked twenty miles overnight just to try to get a viewing spot for this race,' said Otho gleefully. 'All I can say is, they'll be lucky. There isn't a single seat left in the Circus! There are blue tunics everywhere, it's the first time in almost a year that I've seen as many Blues as Greens in the crowd.' He looked me up and down critically. 'Is that what she's wearing? Can't it be blue?'

I had on my mother's white tunic underneath my leather breastplate. Corinna had mended the frayed gold thread on the hem and sleeves and added even more so that it glittered when it caught the light. I wore the gold arm band that Helvia had given me and the little figure of Tigris hung from Anna's ribbon along with a pouch containing my mother's lock of hair.

'She's a princess. Princesses wear whatever they like,' said Scorpus, giving my hand a final slap. He handed me a helmet. It was lined with felt and had a bright gold 'S' painted on it.

'Where did this come from?' I asked.

'I had it made for you at the best tan yard in the city. It's the finest quality leather you can get.'

I put it on carefully over my hair which Corinna had arranged neatly for me that morning.

'Fits perfectly,' I said, doing up the strap. Scorpus smiled.

'Have you got your knife?'

I patted the pocket at the front of my breastplate.

'Good. I won't come with you to the warm-up area. It's better if we're not seen together. As soon as the race is over, Otho's going to smuggle you out of the city and put you on one of his own ships back to Utica. Princess Sophonisba will disappear and no one will be any the wiser about who she is.'

Otho insisted on going out first to announce me and to 'get the crowd going', as he put it.

'My friends,' we heard him shouting above the noise. 'It gives me great pleasure to introduce to you my newest recruit... Queen Sophonisba of the Blues!'

'I'm a queen now,' I said to Scorpus, trying to hide how terrified I felt. 'I keep going up in the world.'

I suddenly realised that he was shaking as much as I was.

'Scorpus? What is it?'

'I'm afraid, Dido. I don't want to lose her all over again.'

I didn't know what to say. Outside the crowd was cheering. Scorpus took a deep breath then put both hands on my shoulders.

'Listen to me,' he said, looking me intently in the eye. 'I know she's watching and so is Antonius. They'll be willing you on at every stride and so will I. You can do this, Dido. You understand me?'

I blinked and nodded.

There was a huge roar as I came out of the changing room. The Forum was packed and for once all heads were turned in the direction of the Blue stables. Moments later, there was an even louder cheer as the Four Winds were led out of their stall.

They looked magnificent, their hard chestnut coats shining like silk, peacock-blue ribbons fluttering from their manes and tails.

'Do they pass inspection, Your Majesty?' asked Atticus, who was standing at their heads, wearing the Blues stable uniform. He had grown a thick brown beard to disguise himself in case Macro or the Praetorians should be watching. Two months of meals from Helvia's cook had added flesh to his bones but he was still a gaunt shadow of the massive figure who had been my father's friend.

'Yes. They'll do. Good plaits,' I said.

The Blues' supporters were pushing, keen for a glimpse of the faction's most famous team, seemingly returned from the dead. We made our way to the warm-up area, a gaggle of people following us. Nicias hadn't arrived, so I circled the Four Winds alone under the critical scrutiny of the spectators packed three lines deep against the guard rope. I got some heckles but I also felt the mood in the crowd change as they watched me drive. It was tempting to show off the Four Winds' pace, but I knew Scorpus would berate me for wasting their energy.

A swarm of Green supporters were now pouring down the path from the stables. Nicias charged through the middle of them at a fast canter. Porcellus and his teammates looked as if they should be pulling Pluto's chariot through the underworld. Their coats gleamed like black marble. We circled each other on opposite sides of the warm-up area. Nicias didn't so much as glance in my direction. The stewards appeared with their urn and approached Nicias first. One of them held their fingers to the crowd and shouted 'Five'. The urn was then offered to me.

'Seven!' yelled the steward as the little blue ball dropped out. A great cheer went up from the Green supporters. Nicias had the inside advantage.

'First dirty trick of the day,' said Atticus, coming to do the final chariot check while one of the Green grooms did the same for Nicias. 'You'll be lucky if rigging the lane draw is the worst of it.'

He checked my wheels one last time.

'Remember. It's all about the turns. Control the pace. Save your horses' strength for when you need it. Good luck, Princess. I'll see you at the finish.'

The spectators scattered, scrambling to get inside the Circus and find their seats, while the Circus officials loaded us into the gates.

Boreas took a dislike to a steward but with some help from Atticus, we got them in. The doors clanged shut behind us. It was strangely quiet. Usually I could hear the noise of eleven other charioteers exchanging jokes and insults as their horses stamped and snorted in feverish anticipation. But Nicias and I hadn't looked at each other once and our teams had become still and alert, as though they understood what was staked on the outcome of the race. I let my eyes slide to the left and saw Porcellus giving me a sidelong look of his own.

'I know it's you in there, man-girl,' said Nicias softly.

I stiffened but didn't look at him. Zephyr's ears pointed forward as he peered into the Circus with interest, as if remembering the last time he'd been here.

'Knew it the moment they told me the Blues were putting up a girl to race. I always dreamed I'd get the chance to teach you a lesson one day. Now I finally get to watch you spill your blood.'

The noise from the crowd was building and I knew they were about to start the countdown. I turned and looked him right in the eye.

'This is for Icarus.'

I planted my feet and took a deep breath.

XLIX

We were neck and neck out of the starting gate. Eight horses fighting for position, their heads nodding in perfect unison. The Circus roared like a mountain erupting. Something landed in the base of my chariot as we raced down the first straight. It was a piece of wood, studded with nails. I kicked it out. Nicias took the first turn at breakneck speed, holding the inside line. I eased the Four Winds towards the middle of the track to avoid the dust cloud coming from Nicias's wheels. For the first lap, we held position.

As the dolphin came down, Nicias increased the pace. Scorpus's advice not to let him build too big a gap echoed in my head. All around the Circus, the Blue and Green supporters were on their feet. Their passion pulsed through the stadium as they sang faction songs and chanted the names of the two inside horses, trying to drown the other side out. As we passed the pits, I saw Caligula standing among the Greens. He was smiling broadly. Praetorians in white uniform flanked him. Thrown by the sight, I misjudged the next turn and Boreas slipped.

'Steady, steady boy.' *Idiot. Don't lose concentration now*. The gap between me and Nicias had increased by half a length and another missile flew past my head. I cracked my whip over Eurus and Auster's ears, looking to regain ground. Then I saw the small water boy standing on the edge of the channel. He looked nervous but determined. Something about the scared look on his face made me swerve instinctively as he hurled the contents of his bucket. Some of it splashed my left arm. I screamed as I smelled hot oil. It felt as if something was eating through my flesh. Up ahead, another water boy stepped on to the track. He paused to adjust his grip on the bucket. I raised my uninjured whip hand, cracked the lash as hard as I could and steered straight for him.

'Go on, go on!' I yelled.

The four chestnut heads came up. Boreas bared his teeth as he charged towards the boy who leaped out of the way just in time, dropping the bucket over his feet. I heard yelps of pain behind me which were quickly snuffed by the cheers of the Blues' supporters.

The golden nose of the third dolphin dropped. Nicias was two chariot lengths clear. I saw Scorpus in the Blue pit, Parmenion and Antigonus either side of him. Scorpus and Antigonus were clenching their fists, urging me on, while Parmenion banged a drum above his head in time with the Blues' supporters' chants. Cries of 'Incitatus' and 'Zephyr' rang throughout the Circus like shields clashing. Zephyr's head crept alongside that of Nicias's rope horse. We were almost back on level terms and shielded from whatever ambush might come from the remaining water boys on the channel. The next turn was approaching. I prepared to pass on the outside.

A hit from Nicias's wheels made me lose my footing. I quickly regained it, but he steered into me again, his face red with hatred. I fell back, nursing my throbbing left arm. Doubt took hold in my mind. I thought of the agony of being shipwrecked in my last race and Icarus lying on the track. Nicias raised his whip. Porcellus and the other three immediately increased their pace, taking them a good five lengths clear before I could gather myself to respond. Caligula's smirking face loomed from the Green pit. Four laps down. Three to go.

I took a risk on the turn into the fifth lap, cutting straight across the corner. Scorpus would have crucified me if I had done it in training. But Zephyr took it magnificently and the crowd roared. I could feel the little wooden carving of Tigris catch under my mother's tunic. The surge in support from the crowd seemed to lift the Four Winds. They stretched their noses, their blue-ribboned manes flying in the wind. The distance between Nicias's chariot and mine closed to four lengths. Then three. Two. The pain in my burned arm was excruciating, but I felt as if I was feeding off of it, drawing strength from it.

The fifth dolphin plummeted. Two laps to go. As he turned for the start of the sixth, Nicias shook his right arm as if he was brandishing his whip. Zephyr took the turn brilliantly, but as his head curled round the corner, I saw something glinting in the sunlight on the track. I yanked on the right rein and Zephyr's hooves just missed the row of silver nails pointing skyward like the teeth of a boar-trap.

Nicias looked over his shoulder to see if his trick had worked. The action put him off balance and he veered slightly off course, away from the channel. I saw the gap and I swear Boreas did too. Nostrils flared, he put on a burst of speed which his teammates matched, and we overtook on the inside. The wheels of the two chariots sent sparks flying. The Four Winds pulled into a one-length lead.

My hair had escaped from inside my helmet and whipped around my face. The noise of the crowd was deafening, and I strained to hear the drumming of hooves behind me. Were they getting louder or fainter? Did I have enough of a lead? Should I put in the final push now or wait? The channel was blocking my view of Scorpus. I'd have given anything for him to tell me what to do. Silently, I begged my father for help.

The last dolphin was down. Approaching the turning post for the final lap, a groom in a green uniform who had been picking nails out of the sand dived for cover. The drumming of hooves grew louder. Porcellus's head passed me and I sensed Nicias on my shoulder. I fought to hold on, knowing that I had the advantage of the inside line. But a sinking realisation was setting in. My horses were tiring. Six months out of Circus racing had taken its toll. They were brave, magnificent horses, but they weren't the team they had once been. We didn't have enough speed to hold the lead for the finish.

Porcellus, on the other hand, looked as fresh as he had at the start of the race. We were half-way to the last turn and his head was level with Boreas's. There was some eyeballing between them, a bumping of shoulders. But Boreas was too exhausted to make more of a contest of it. The younger, stronger horse had the beating of him.

Little by little, I felt the wheels of my chariot beginning to turn into the channel. Nicias was steering into me. I fought to hold the line, but his chariot was nudging against mine, knocking it off course like a hammer tapping on a nail. The space ahead of me was narrowing. If I slowed down, the race was lost. There was no escape and within a few strides the wheels of my chariot would shatter against the hard wall of the channel. Fearfully, I glanced at Nicias. His eyes were fixed on my chariot, his teeth gritted in deadly concentration.

A sliver of sand appeared between the edge of his chariot and mine. Nicias swore and flexed his left arm as he tried closing the gap again. But I could still see the sand between us. Swinging wildly with his whip, Nicias aimed his lash at Porcellus. I realised what was happening. The three outside horses in Nicias's team were obeying his command, but Porcellus was holding them off. The muscles in his neck and shoulders were bulging with the effort. He was stopping Nicias from driving me into the channel.

The last turn was upon us. We were going fast, too fast, but if I slowed down, the race was lost. I waited, frantically trying to judge it right, praying for someone to guide my hand. I pulled hard. The

Four Winds' noses curved beautifully around the turn, Porcellus and his teammates shadowing them on the right. Nicias was trying with all his might to drag his team to the left, forcing the shipwreck. But Porcellus wouldn't yield. I came off the turn with the slight advantage. There was half a length of track between us and the finish. Crouching as low as I could, I gave Boreas, Eurus, Auster and Zephyr their heads. Eight magnificent horses – four chestnut, four black – streaked towards the finish. We crossed it.

The crowd was chanting something. I couldn't tell what it was at first.

'Sophonisba! Sophonisba!'

People were streaming on to the track. Supporters in Blue tunics were pursuing me around the Circus. I eased the Four Winds to a canter and gave them a loose rein. They were blowing hard but to my relief, showed no sign of injury. I grabbed Tigris and the pouch with my mother's lock of hair and pressed them both to my lips. Pulling up on the Blues' side of the Circus, I saluted to Otho, who was on his feet, clenching his fists and celebrating in front of cheering supporters. I waved to Helvia who was standing beside him, her face wreathed in a smile. A swarm of drivers, engineers and grooms spilled out of the pit and surrounded us. Parmenion hauled himself aboard my chariot and kissed me. Antigonus and Helix were there too, both applauding. The chant of 'Sophonisba!' continued to ring out through the Circus. I searched the crowd, looking for the person I wanted to see above all. At last I found him. Scorpus wore a look of pride that made my heart feel as if it might explode. I pointed to the 'S' on my helmet and he nodded.

Then I saw Nicias. He had pulled up in front of the Greens' pit. Two of their grooms had gone to the black horses' sweating heads. Nicias stepped down from the back of the chariot and tore off his gold helmet. Our eyes met across the celebrating crowd of Blues' supporters. I watched his hand go to the pocket in the front of his breastplate. He took out the knife concealed inside it.

I flung off Parmenion's arm and jumped down from the chariot.

'Stop him!' I screamed. 'Stop him!'

One of the grooms tried to grab Nicias as he approached the horses' heads but after a short tussle, the groom was flung aside, clutching a bloodied arm. Nicias advanced on Porcellus who reared, shaking off the other groom's hold, punching out with his forelegs. I tried to fight my way through the crowd, but they wouldn't let me. I wasn't going to get there in time.

But another figure in a green tunic was racing across the sand, six Praetorians working hard to keep up with him.

Caligula grabbed Nicias as he tried to plunge the blade of his knife into Porcellus's eye. Flinging Nicias to the ground, he started to kick him. Nicias began to crawl away, but the Praetorians surrounded him, blocking his escape. Caligula kept up his assault. Blood spattered across the yellow sand as Nicias's mouth turned crimson. Caligula's fine hair became dishevelled. A chill of silence descended over the Circus. All eyes were transfixed by the scene in front of the Greens' pit. Slowly, Nicias stopped struggling to get up and the fingers holding the knife went limp.

Caligula aimed one last kick into Nicias's chest. He wiped his forehead and then walked down the track towards me, while two of the Praetorians dragged away Nicias's unconscious body. The emperor looked out of breath but otherwise calm. A pale hand extended itself towards me, a great emerald ring glowing on the middle finger.

'Congratulations, Princess. A most exhilarating race. I think I may have found a new lead charioteer for the Greens.'

He took my wrist and held my arm up in the air. After a long pause, there were a few claps which gradually spread throughout the Circus. Some people stayed silent, though. Many were Blues' supporters. But I saw some Greens refusing to applaud as well.

Frantically, I looked for Scorpus but the Praetorians had formed a wall around me. Cassius Chaerea was one of them. His face was unreadable. Porcellus was being led away. It needed the combined efforts of eight Green grooms to restrain him.

'Let's take you to your new home, shall we?' said Caligula.

L

I collapsed against the wall, trying to get my breath. The door just wouldn't open. For all of Caligula's pretended hospitality, he clearly knew that I would run the moment I had the chance.

They'd brought me to a luxurious bedroom at the Greens' club-house, three times the size of my own, with beautiful paintings on the walls like in Otho and Helvia's quarters. But I felt as if the crimson room was closing in on me, slowly squeezing the air from my chest. Nicias's clothes were still in a careless pile at the foot of the bed. There were other traces of him too. On the wall by the door was a single laurel wreath, its leaves dry and shrivelled. I guessed that it was the first he'd ever won at the Circus. For all that I hated him, somehow that faded wreath made me see something in Nicias that I could recognise in myself. I wondered where he was now and what was going to happen to him.

I went to the window and pressed my face into the narrow opening to see if there was anyone on the street that I could call to. But the crowd of Green supporters that usually thronged outside the main gate wasn't there. A bitter tang of smoke filled the air and I tasted something else too, something restless and violent. Men were running past in pairs and groups, some of them carrying sticks and torches. I could hear shouts and fights breaking out.

I went to the door and tried tugging the handle again. It wouldn't budge and my arm hurt too much to give it more effort. A female slave had smeared cream on the burned skin before bandaging it. On the bed were the clothes she had brought me, an armful of silks in bright colours. *From the emperor*, she had said quietly. If he thought I was going to race for him, become a toy like Nicias... I picked up a dress and started to shred it, pulling out the silver thread.

Hearing footsteps in the corridor outside, I stopped, breathless. The key rattled in the lock and the door opened.

Justus put his finger to his lips and beckoned.

'Quickly. Follow me.'

He led me down the long, painted corridor and a winding set of stairs. We crossed another corridor and entered a richly furnished room which looked like someone's study. There was a door that led outside. Now I realised where we were. It was Ruga's private garden. There was the fig tree where Justus and I had once stood together, looking for the green bird. Beneath the tree, a black horse was grazing by the light of the moon, plucking greedily at the grass. An old man was clutching his lead-rope in one hand and leaning on a walking stick with the other.

'We're here, Uncle Ruga. Thank you,' said Justus.

I ran to Porcellus and flung my arms around him, breathing in his warm, sweet smell as if it were air in my lungs. He let me hold him, pressing his chin gently into my back. Then I felt him sniffing hopefully at my tunic, searching for a fig. I laughed and when I showed him I didn't have anything, he wrinkled his nose and blew softly at me. Then he went back to plucking at the fresh grass which he hadn't tasted for so long.

Ruga peered at me.

'Is this your horse?'

'Yes. He's mine. Thank you for holding him.'

'My pleasure. Splendid animal.' Ruga patted Porcellus's neck.

Justus was unlocking the gate that led to the narrow alleyway outside.

'Come on,' he hissed. I dragged a reluctant Porcellus to a cart covered in a huge piece of heavy linen. It looked like a builder's wagon. Atticus was standing next to it.

'Atticus!' I exclaimed. 'How did you...?'

'Your friend here came to find Scorpus and me after the race. You can thank him later. Now help me with this.'

Between us, Atticus and I quickly hitched the cart to Porcellus, who kept trying to go back to the grass in the garden. To keep him quiet, I picked some figs from the tree and gave them to Ruga to feed to him, which he did with the delight of a small child.

'How did you think of all of this?' I asked Justus as we frantically fastened the reins.

'I only got you this far. The cart was their idea.'

'What's one more rubbish cart in a city that's full of them?' said Atticus. 'No one noticed Boreas. Why would they notice the most famous racehorse in the city? Now come on, let's get you out of here.'

Justus and I lay hidden under the linen cloth. The cart jolted through the streets. We could hear shouting and people running.

'What's happening?' I asked.

'There's a lot of unrest in the city. The emperor has been losing support for months and after what happened in the Circus today, things are worse. There's a riot going on in the poorer part of the city. People are angry about Nicias. He was a hero to the Green supporters.'

'Do you know what they did with him?'

'He's in the sanatorium but whether he'll survive his injuries, I don't know.'

The cart turned sharply to the right. I rolled into Justus and he held me steady. I didn't move away, and he left his hand on my shoulder.

'Charicles is dead,' he said after a pause.

'What happened?'

'Caligula chased him into the feed room and stabbed him. It was awful, like watching a rat being cornered by a dog.'

'I don't understand how you got Porcellus out of there.'

'Caligula took the guards off his door tonight and ordered him to be put in an ordinary stall. He's as angry with Porcellus as he is with Nicias. I think he might have had him killed if we hadn't got him out.'

'But how did you manage him by yourself?'

'He's always been quite calm with me. Maybe because he remembers me as a friend of yours.'

The cart made another turn.

'What do you think will happen when they discover we're gone?' I asked.

'They'll come after us, I should think. But I'm hoping they don't notice for a while. The Praetorians are a little distracted.'

'Because of the riots?'

'No. Because they don't have a commanding prefect.'

'*What?* What happened to Macro?'

'Your winning today signed his death warrant. Caligula wants to be his own master now.'

'You mean Macro's dead?'

'Not yet. Right now, he's on his way to Egypt. He thinks he's being made governor there, as compensation for having the command of the guard taken from him. But some soldiers are following him.'

'Will they really kill their own commander?'

'They won't have to. He'll be expected to do the honourable thing.'

I tried to see his face in the dark.

'What about Ennia? What's going to happen to her?'

'She's staying with a friend. I made sure she was safe.'

The cart suddenly jolted again. Justus peered out.

'We're here.'

A strong scent overwhelmed me and I realised that I was once more in the familiar surroundings of the docks beside the river Tiber. Porcellus snorted at the sight of the water. There were only a few barges and transports moored to the quay. Looking up from the deck of one was a face I knew.

'I'll be,' said Rufus, shaking his head. 'It *is* you, Dido. The man didn't lie.'

I turned to Atticus in amazement.

'You told Scorpus about how they helped you,' he said. 'So he knew he could trust them to take you back again. Otho's paid them a good sum for their trouble.'

Mathos and Abascantus were opening the entry bay into the hull. The slope from street level to the loading dock was slippery but I coaxed Porcellus down it, with Mathos in front, shaking a bucket of grain, and together we secured him inside the boat's shallow hold.

I ran back up and hugged Atticus.

'How are the Four Winds?'

'Not a scratch on them. Otho's invited me to stay with the Blues. Now that he doesn't have a trainer, he'd like me to help out. So I'll take good care of your horses, Dido, don't you worry. Promised Scorpus the same thing.'

'Where is Scorpus?'

'He'll follow you to Utica with Parmenion and Antigonus when things have settled. It will look suspicious if you all disappear on the same night.'

Atticus pressed something in my hand.

'The mistress wanted me to give you this. She said to open it when you get home.'

I took the little box he handed me and gave him another hug before turning to Justus.

'Goodbye, Dido,' he said.

'Aren't you coming with me?'

'No.'

'But it's not safe for you here, Justus! They'll find out it was you who helped me get out.'

'I have to go back for Uncle Ruga. It's not safe for him either. And I need to protect Ennia. Caligula won't be satisfied with just Macro's death, he'll want to kill his whole family.'

'But... where will you go?'

He shook his head and smiled.

'I don't know. We'll find somewhere, a long way from Rome. Just like you did. I owe it to them, Dido. I can't leave them.'

I stared into his serious, handsome face. The boy I used to know was still there. But most of him was gone.

'Will you let me know somehow... that you're safe?'

'I'll try.'

I smoothed the dark lock of hair from his brow.

'I always wanted to do that,' I said.

He put his hand up and wrapped his fingers around mine. For a precious moment, it was all there was – the sound of the water and the touch of his hand.

Then Atticus swore.

'Praetorian scum. Damn it.' He was looking towards the far end of the street.

'You have to go,' said Justus. 'Go on, Dido, go!'

He pushed me away and I jumped on to the boat's deck.

'Praetorians! Quick, we have to cast off.'

'Praetorians again? They do seem to follow you,' grumbled Mathos. He hurried to untie the mooring ropes, but Rufus stopped him.

'The wind's dropped. They'll see us for sure, we'll be stranded in the open. Quick, in here.'

He pulled open the trap-door set into the deck. I looked for Atticus and Justus but they had gone. Rufus pushed me down the ladder into the cargo hold and he and Mathos quickly followed. I went to Porcellus, who didn't like the black confines of the space and was resisting Abascantus's efforts to calm him.

'Quiet that horse!' said Mathos.

The decking boards above us creaked. Rufus put a finger to his lips. None of us moved a muscle. Porcellus's eyes were wide and his head rigid, but he didn't make a sound. The boards creaked again. A shaft of moonlight suddenly flooded into the cargo hold. The trap-door was open. Someone was looking at us.

'Can you see them, Cassius?' shouted a voice from higher up on the quayside.

Cassius Chaerea's blue eyes were bright and unblinking. They rested for a long moment on Porcellus and me.

'No. They're not here. Let's go.'

The trap-door closed.

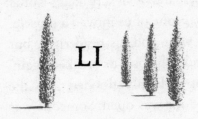

LI

I sat on the long porch, looking over to the mountains in the distance. The sky was turning gold and purple clouds were racing towards the horizon. There was a delicious smell in the air from the huge boar that had been roasting all day in front of the house. Hanno and Abibaal were standing at either end, attempting to turn the spit. They nearly managed to tip it into the fire but after much squabbling, they got the beast on its back. Abibaal came running up the steps.

'I am so hungry,' he announced. 'When are we getting started?'

'As soon as the bride's ready,' I told him.

Abibaal sighed.

'Weddings are so boring,' he said. 'I'm definitely not getting married if this is what you have to go through.'

Hanno came to join us and together we sat looking out at the fields and the sunset. The spring rains had brought out the green in the landscape.

I thought how much I loved it here, how it had come to feel like home. From opposite ends of the pasture closest to the house, Sciron and Porcellus were eyeing each other mistrustfully.

'They're not really friends yet, are they?' asked Hanno.

'Sometimes the best of friendships can take a bit of time,' I replied. 'They'll get there. They need to get used to each other.'

Sciron lowered his head and started to graze. After a while, Porcellus did the same.

'What happened to your moon necklace?' asked Abibaal, pointing to my neck where a fine glass-beaded chain had replaced the frayed ribbon holding Tigris and the pouch with my mother's hair.

'I remembered what you said, about wanting the dead to know that we're still thinking of them. So I left it in Rome for my papa. But that kind woman I told you about gave me this to replace it, see?'

I held out the delicate silver wire so that Abibaal could see it.

'I wish I had lots of money and could buy myself any jewel I wanted,' he said. 'Do the charioteers at the Circus wear lots of jewellery? Parmenion says that Nicias had a gold helmet.'

'You'll have to get to the Circus and win lots of races so you can buy one.'

Scorpus came on to the porch.

'Dido. Anna wants you. She's ready.'

I went into the cool of the house and down the corridor to our little room next to the kitchen. Anna was wearing a white woollen dress with a yellow belt. Her hair was braided and she was smiling from ear to ear.

'You look beautiful,' I said and kissed her. She linked her arm through mine, and I led her back out to the porch where Parmenion and Antigonus were now waiting alongside Scorpus and the boys. I took Anna over to Antigonus, who looked happier than I'd ever seen him. Then I stepped back as Scorpus clasped their hands together.

Parmenion, who was next to me, gave me a knowing look.

'Thinking about your friend?'

I looked out to the horizon. I *had* been thinking about him. But not quite in the way that Parmenion meant.

'I was just... thinking about the way people change. And how they can stay the same, in a way. Does that make sense?'

Parmenion tugged on a strand of my hair which was starting to turn blonde again. Antigonus was now slipping a ring on Anna's finger.

'Can't see you doing that. Getting married,

breeding little man-girls,' said Parmenion. 'So what now?'

'I'm not sure,' I admitted. 'The only dream I've ever had is to race at the Circus Maximus. Now that I've done it, all I can think about is going back and winning again. But so long as Caligula's emperor, I don't see how I can.'

Antigonus was picking Anna up and carrying her down the steps. Hanno and Abibaal ran after them, throwing handfuls of nuts and rose petals and shrieking with enthusiasm. Scorpus opened two pitchers of wine and started pouring them into a row of drinking cups.

'What about you, what are you going to do?' I said to Parmenion. 'Do you want to return to the Circus some day?'

'If this leg ever properly heals.' Parmenion flexed his knee. It still didn't straighten. 'Otho said I'd be welcome back at the Blues any time. I've got to hope, haven't I? Just one time in my life, I'd like to hear that crowd shouting my name. You know?'

I nodded. I did know.

Did any of this really happen?

Dido, the heroine of this story, exists only in my imagination and there is no evidence that girls were ever allowed to compete in chariot races in ancient Rome. At this time, being a girl almost always meant staying at home, not getting much education or exercise, and learning to be a good wife and mother. But I'm certain there were young girls like Dido who watched the races at the great Circus Maximus stadium and dreamed of becoming famous charioteers themselves. We know that Roman girls were big fans of the races, just like their brothers and fathers. Tokens from chariot-racing events have been found in Roman girls' graves, which is a bit like a football-mad girl today being buried with a ticket stub from an Arsenal–Liverpool football match.

Dido herself may be fictional, but several of the other characters in this book are real people from history and many of the details about them are based on descriptions by Roman writers. The emperor Caligula, for example, genuinely was an obsessive fan of both chariot racing and the Green faction. He liked to dine and sometimes even spend the night at the Green stables and he famously had a favourite racehorse called Incitatus, which was provided with its own marble stable and a jewelled collar. When Caligula succeeded his great-uncle Tiberius as emperor in the year AD37 it was rumoured that he had murdered Tiberius with the help of the head of the Praetorian Guard, Sutorius Macro and a doctor called Charicles – who in my book becomes the man who helps the Greens win by using his knowledge of a plant called ephedron, which was actually used by ancient athletes to improve their performance.

Another historical character in the book is Cassius Chaerea. He served in the Roman army under Caligula's father and later became a tribune in the Praetorian Guard. Caligula is said to have made fun of him for his high-pitched speaking voice. Not only was this typical of the young emperor's cruelty, it earned him a dangerous enemy in Cassius Chaerea.

Acknowledgements

I am so lucky to have met my agent Nancy Miles whose response to the manuscript for this book was the stuff of dreams. My wonderful editors, Fiona Kennedy and Lauren Atherton, have championed Dido's story and shown me how to make it better. Levente Szabo designed the beautiful cover with oversight from art director Jessie Price. Thank you so much to them and everyone at Zephyr/Head of Zeus who has helped along the way.

I relied heavily on the work of many scholars in creating the world of *Circus Maximus* but would like to single out Fik Meijer, whose book *Chariot Racing in the Roman Empire* was an invaluable guide. The Hellenic and Roman Library in London supplied me with almost everything else I needed and was a lovely place to study. Professor Dr. Mario Thevis of the German Sport University in

Cologne was probably startled to get an email out of the blue from a woman in England wanting to know about plausible methods of drugging horses in the ancient world, but he responded helpfully to my queries as did Dr. Jason König. James Wall, Classicist and world's greatest school trip organiser, read the manuscript for me and shared photos of Tunisia.

My fellow teachers at Port Regis School have given me great support and encouragement over the years. I'd like to issue a shout out to a group who are not just good women but good friends – Kate de Bono, Julia Cardozo, Naomi Dickins, Rebecca Eves, Theresa Latham, Barbara Lonergan and Emma Webb – and to say drinks and crisps at the Grosvenor are on me when this comes out. Also invited is James Webb, for generously organising my timetable so that I can write in the afternoons. Thank you as ever, with all my heart, to the UL Tea Support Group – Aude, Daniel, Katie and Miriam – and to my family in Dorset and Bermuda. The last couple of years have been pretty tough for my father and I just want to say to him – Daddy, I love you very much, you are the original Freeze and the world's greatest dancer. (Watch me now…!)

My greatest debt, as ever, is to my husband,

Julian. He always believes in me, even when I am struggling to believe in myself. Without him I would be lost, in every sense of the word.

Annelise Gray
Dorset
March 2021

Dido's adventure continues in

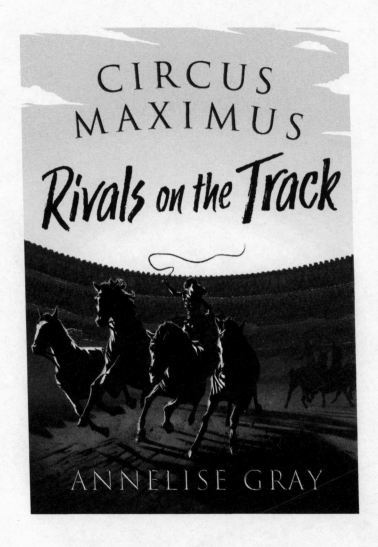

CIRCUS
MAXIMUS
Rivals on the Track

ANNELISE GRAY

Read the first chapter now.

I

'Faster, come on boy, faster! We've got to get inside them at the turn!'

Porcellus's black ears were braced against the wind like shields raised for battle. His neck was tense, his bright eyes wide with excitement.

'Come on!'

The gap to the lead chariot was closing. Porcellus's flying hooves ate up the ground and my opponent looked fearfully over his shoulder. Thought you had the beating of us, didn't you? I smiled. But you underestimated me, my friend. Just like they all do. The other charioteer lashed his team's tiring rumps with the leather tongue of his whip. But it was too little, too late. Porcellus slid past them, curling around the turning post like a serpent. I felt the wind dragging through my hair as we galloped down the last straight. The finish line was in sight. The Circus crowd was on their feet, roaring us home.

'Dido!' they chanted. 'Dido, Dido, Dido...'

'Dido!'

The roar faded from my ears and the excited faces lining the walls of the Circus Maximus disappeared along with the great stadium itself. It was just Porcellus and I on the practice track at my Uncle Scorpus's stable, racing for glory against an imaginary rival. But a lone voice was still calling my name.

'Dido!'

Scorpus was marching across the pasture. He looked furious and I knew why. I hauled back on the reins and Porcellus obeyed the command to slow down, snatching irritably at the bit in his mouth. The wheels of my light training chariot crunched to a halt as Scorpus reached us.

'What do you think you're doing? Do you want people to see you?'

He pointed to the top of the valley, above the stables, where travellers passed along the coast road on their way to the nearby town of Utica.

'No one's going to get a good look at us from up there,' I said. 'Calm down, Scorpus, I was only giving Porcellus a run.'

'You're not even wearing a helmet! Has it slipped your mind that the emperor probably has half the Roman army out there, looking for a girl charioteer? And that you're driving a stolen horse?'

My hackles went up.

'Porcellus isn't stolen. He's mine, my father gave him to me.'

'I'm not sure that's how the emperor would see it.'

'You know how much I love Porcellus.' I was getting angry now. 'I'd never do anything to risk losing him again. But it's not fair to keep him locked in his stable all day. He's not even allowed to join the other horses when they come out here for training. It's like when he was racing for the Greens, with Emperor Caligula keeping him chained up as if he was a pet dog.'

'So you're comparing me to Caligula now?'

'No. You're a bit less of a tyrant. But only a bit.'

I saw a reluctant smile tugging at the corner of his mouth and I felt better. I hated it when we argued.

'Honestly, Scorpus, where's the harm? It's been two months since Porcellus and I escaped from Rome. In that whole time, no one has come here looking for us. No one.'

'Well, that's where you're wrong. They just did. That's why I came out to warn you.'

Fear bubbled in my stomach.

'What do you mean? Who?'

'A messenger. He came from Rome. Bringing this.'

It was a picture, roughly painted on a square of yellow papyrus. Scorpus handed it to me and I studied the image of a female figure in a white tunic trimmed with gold. Her long dark hair flowed from under the helmet and in her raised hand was a whip. She was driving a chariot pulled by a galloping black horse with a white star clearly visible on his forehead.

'It's me at the Circus Maximus,' I said. 'When I raced for the Blues as Princess Sophonisba. And that's Porcellus.'

'Yes. And it came with this letter from Otho.' Scorpus held up another piece of papyrus. The red wax seal on its edge was broken. 'Get Porcellus back to the stable, then come inside and I'll read it to you.'

'What does it say? Wait, read it to me now, what does it say? Scorpus!'

'Horses first,' he said walking back across the pasture towards the house.

I unhitched Porcellus from the chariot, leaped on to his back and galloped him to the stables. We passed Scorpus's one-time apprentice and now assistant trainer, Antigonus, who gave us a brief wave. As soon as we reached the barn, Scorpus's old favourite, Sciron, ambled over to the gate. He'd been retired from the circus track a long time when I first met him and his dark brown muzzle was now heavily speckled with grey. Porcellus whickered at him in greeting. Sciron was the only friend he'd made since he got here.

Quickly I rubbed Porcellus down before putting

him in his stall. More horses had come up to the pasture fence, and although I was in a hurry to find out what was in Scorpus's letter, I went and gave their noses a rub. The red roan, Cupid, tried to hold me up by fastening his teeth onto my tunic pocket, where I sometimes kept sticky dates as a treat. From his stall, Porcellus screeched in protest. He regarded those dates as his special privilege.

Parmenion limped around the corner from the feed room, a bucket in his hand. He was still carrying the knee injury from his crash in the Circus months before and couldn't manage much more than stable duties. His tawny hair was sticking up as usual and his sun-bronzed face was shiny with sweat. Porcellus's mood changed at once. His ears flapped forward and he kicked his door in excitement.

'Hello, you impatient viper. And hello to you too, Porcellus.' Parmenion grinned at me as he opened the door of Porcellus's stall.

'Very funny. Did you remember to put some olive oil in with his feed?'

'I certainly did, Princess.'

I rolled my eyes.

'Haven't you got tired of that joke yet?'

'I don't seem to have done, no.'

'Why that girl at the bakery likes you, I will never understand. You won't forget to fill up Porcellus's water, will you? It's hot in there and he's not going to get out again until nightfall.'

By the door which led into the kitchen, my young cousins, Hanno and Abibaal, were lingering beside the domed baking oven. A delicious smell of warm bread filled the air. Anna was making lunch for everyone. Through the open door, I could see her, her black hair escaping from its long plait and her teeth clenched as she heaved a vast pot towards the fire.

'Offer to help, you idiots,' I scolded the boys. 'She's got a baby inside her, remember. Antigonus would be furious if he saw you letting his wife lift a heavy thing on her own like that.'

I found Scorpus in the little room where he did his accounts. He was sitting at a table, studying the square of crumpled papyrus. I saw the worry in his black eyes. My heart thudded uncomfortably.

'Is it... bad news?' I asked.

He sighed and started to read.

My good friend,

I write this in haste. Helvia and I leave Rome tonight and there is little time, but much to tell you. You need to know, first of all, that I have sold the Blue faction and therefore our business relationship – though not, I hope, our friendship

– must come to an end, for now at least. Betucius Barus will be the new faction master. I've told him you're the best trainer in the empire and that he'd be mad not to continue to buy horses from you. But Betucius favours the Spanish breeds over the African and I fear you may see fewer scouts from the Blues coming by than you used to. I know this will affect your livelihood and I am sorry.

The reasons for our sudden departure will not surprise you. The emperor is in ill humour. Ever since the humiliating defeat of his favourite driver at the Circus Maximus by the mystery charioteer, known only as Princess Sophonisba, Caligula has brooded with all the petulance of a child who has lost his favourite toy. He can never stomach the Green faction being defeated of course. But he was keen to make the girl their new star so that he could fawn over her as he once did your former apprentice Nicias. That she should flee Rome rather than accept the honour of that invitation, he regards as an insufferable insult.

Caligula's advisors try to divert his mind. There is talk that the Greens have recruited a new driver, a precocious young talent who will arrive in Rome soon and hopefully restore some of the emperor's good humour. But the emperor nurses a grudge like a bloodhound guards a bone. He is determined to discover the princess's true identity and force her to return to Rome, along with the racehorse she stole from under his nose. To that end, he sends the Praetorian Guard almost daily to the Blues' clubhouse to intimidate me. The water is a little hot for my liking. It seems prudent to remove myself from Rome.

Please, my friend, do not be concerned for me. I have many friends around the empire and I shall build my fortune again elsewhere. Helvia is here now and tells me the boat is about to leave and I must finish writing. She bids me pass on her fond wishes to the princess.

I trust we will meet again. Until then, may the gods protect you.

Your friend,
Opellius Otho

Scorpus finished reading and looked up at me. I sank onto a low stool. Scorpus came around the table and squatted in front of me.

'They'll be safe, Dido, I promise.'

'You don't know that. What if Caligula finds them and kills them?' I was struggling to speak. 'It'll be because of me, because they were protecting me.'

'He won't find them. They've got Otho's money and Helvia's cunning. That'll be more than enough to keep them out of trouble.'

My breathing steadied.

'What about you though, Scorpus? How are you going to make a living if you can't sell horses to the Blues anymore?'

'You can let me worry about that. I'll think of something. There's always the Red or White faction, although they don't send so many scouts this way. I'd rather not sell to the Greens, what with them being the emperor's favourite team. But, if there's no other choice, we'll see. It's you I'm worried about.'

He picked up the picture of me and Porcellus.

'This is a reward poster,' he explained. 'The emperor's offering ten million sesterces to anyone who can find you and Porcellus and bring you back to Rome.'

'Ten million?' I was astounded. 'That must be more prize money than the Green faction wins at the Circus in a year!'

'Probably. Just shows how much you're worth to him, Dido.'

'What do you think he would do to me? If I had

to go back?'

Scorpus hesitated.

'I can't be sure. He might want to punish you for taking Porcellus. Caligula thinks of the horse as his own, even if he belonged to you first. But my best guess is he'd try to make you race for the Greens, as he intended before.'

I shook my head violently.

'Never. I won't ever do that. Not while the emperor's their biggest supporter. He's the reason my father's dead and he killed Icarus and I'll never forgive him. Never.'

'Well, now you know why I wanted you to stay out of sight.'

I hung my head. Scorpus squeezed my shoulder.

'I know, Dido. I know it's not been easy. You're a charioteer in your blood. You want to be out there, tearing around the track at a circus again. There is an obvious solution, you know.'

'You mean go back to being Leon.'

He nodded. I sighed in frustration.

'That means starting again at the beginning, competing at the local games in Utica.' I tapped the poster in his hand. 'I won at the Circus Maximus, Scorpus! I had hundreds of thousands of people screaming my name! Well, not my name. But they were cheering for me all the same.'

'They also cheered for you at the Circus when you raced for the Blues as Leon.'

'I know. But when I was Princess Sophonisba, I was allowed to be a girl so I was a little bit myself. When I'm Leon, I have to be a boy, somebody completely different. I have to keep my hair short and put on that dye Anna makes for me and not speak too much. It's not fair. Why can't I be Dido?'

'You know why,' said Scorpus gently. 'I wish it was different, Dido. But chariot racing is man's world. Always has been, always will be.

Zephyr is an imprint of Head of Zeus.
At Zephyr we are proud to publish books
you can read and re-read time and time
again because they tell a brilliant story
and because they entertain you.

@_ZephyrBooks

@_zephyrbooks

HeadofZeusBooks

www.headofzeus.com

ZEPHYR

THE SUNDAY PHILOSOPHY CLUB

E[...]ch, at[...]ot a[...]m ch[...]he or[...] such as Isabel Dalhousie.

But behind the Georgian façades, Edinburgh's moral compasses are spinning with greed, dishonesty, lust and murderous intent. As the editor of the *Review of Applied Ethics*, Isabel knows all about the difference between good and bad. Which is probably why she is by instinct an amateur sleuth. And instinct tells her the man who tumbled to his death in front of her eyes after a concert in the Usher Hall didn't fall. He was pushed.

With Isabel Dalhousie, Alexander McCall Smith introduces a new and waspish female sleuth to tackle murder, mayhem—and the mysteries of life.